Warwickshire County Council

ent, deftly revealing the mysterious connections between the women and the rather grand dilapidated house that united them'   *Sunday Express*

DISCARDED

'Enticing . . . engaging . . . it has a definite melancholy'

Ireland

'Irresistibly sensational ... a darkly playful tale about beauty, ageing and morality, brought to life by a writing style brimming with witty detail ... This is a book to consume in a single sitting, a packet of biscuits close to hand'

Country Life

'The ladies are likely to linger in your thoughts long after you have put the book down'
Oxford Mail

THE LADIES OF THE HOUSE

Molly McGrann is a literary critic, poet and novelist. A former editor at *The Paris Review*, she is the author of two acclaimed novels, *360 Flip* and *Exurbia*. Originally from the USA, she now lives in Oxfordshire with her family.

Also by Molly McGrann

360 Flip

Exurbia

the LADIES *of the* HOUSE

Molly McGrann

PICADOR

First published 2015 by Picador

First published in paperback 2016 by Picador
an imprint of Pan Macmillan
20 New Wharf Road, London N1 9RR
Associated companies throughout the world
www.panmacmillan.com

ISBN 978-1-4472-7477-3

1 3 5 7 9 8 6 4 2

A CIP catalogue record for this book is available from the British Library.

Printed and bound by CPI Group (UK) Ltd, Croydon, CR0 4YY

Visit **www.picador.com** to read more about all our books
and to buy them. You will also find features, author interviews and
news of any author events, and you can sign up for e-newsletters
so that you're always first to hear about our new releases.

For Mouse

It was a minor item in the newspaper, her last English news-paper, or the last one she would read on English soil. Just the kind of headline to draw her eye: *Three Found Dead in North London*, and then their names. Police were alerted after a woman collapsed outside a home in Primrose Hill and was declared dead at the scene, despite all efforts to revive her. Two more bodies were found inside the house. Neighbours said there were no suspicious circumstances to report, except that they were all dead, all at once. Given the recent high temperatures around the country – such a dry, hot July, the barley blackened, the corn stunted, hens not laying right – early discovery of their bodies was a relief, for the smell of lingering death was not sweet, *not* a fairy-tale ending. 'Unfortunately there was nothing to be done,' said a police spokesman. Other heat-related fatalities had been reported and the hospitals were said to be overflowing.

Marie Gillies had forgotten to breathe. When she did breathe, the feeling of doing so was unfamiliar, as if she had to think to do it. Briefly, she feared she might always have to think about breathing. How would she cope? And when she went to sleep at night, what would happen then?

They were dead.

Heathrow swarmed around her. She thought she would burst with the news but there was no one to tell in the busy terminal, no way to explain that three people she knew – well, she did not *know* them, had never met them, but she had spoken to them on the phone. Quite a lot on the phone. Now they were dead. They were gone.

It must have been the heat, nothing to do with her. Marie stood up. Her hands wanted to be busy. She would have done a bit of tidying, given the chance, or folded linens into identical squares. Cleared out a cupboard, put the ornaments in order, swept the floor. Made a cup of tea. The best she could do was go and wash; her hands were sticky with newsprint. She hated that dusty feeling blunting her fingertips. But where, in the vast hall, was the toilet? There, in the distance – she had to squint to see – was a sign: the usual symbols with an arrow. A big walk for someone in her fifties, clinically obese, whose new shoes were giving her a blister.

'It was the blooming heat that killed them,' Marie murmured, stuffing the newspaper into her handbag. She set off across the terminal, panting all the way. No doubt they had turned up the fire, too, daft and old as they were. Cups of tea going cold upon their knees, biscuits melting into the dregs, mouths agape, fetid breath whistling out. She knew the smell of old people, the cellar scent that slept in the folds of their clothes and behind their ears. 'It was the heat,' Marie said once more – aloud, to be sure.

She was not accustomed to travelling. She had been dazzled at first by the hard white light of the airport and stopped in the middle of everything, taking it in. So many encumbered passengers bumping into one another, stopping and starting, no clear path through the crowd, the terminal blocked by bags and trolleys and families trying to stay together – Marie clung to her boarding card. She had never been anywhere. Her passport was safely zipped away in a nylon sac that hung around her neck, under her blouse, slapping her belly as she stopped and started with the rest of them. Her handbag was brand new, stinking of freshly tanned hide, and she had another bag to carry as well, packed with her toothbrush and a change of clothes and some baby wipes, in case they lost her suitcase. Now she really needed the toilet, and she wanted to get her jumper off – boiling, she was, but how would she manage *that* with her bags to tend to and a boarding card ready to produce at all times? It was too much for Marie. There was hysteria in Britain over unattended luggage, but really, she must drop something. Here came the voice over the tannoy, the polite but firm voice that said, 'Please do not leave baggage unattended at any time.' The voice of Nanny herding children inside and upstairs to the nursery where it was warm and safe, where there was hot chocolate if everyone behaved.

She didn't kill those people. But she felt guilty enough. She needed to get away from the crowd. She dragged her things into the Ladies and pulled off her jumper, quietly cursing when her handbag got wet sitting by the sink while she scrubbed her hands with lashings of liquid soap –

pumping, pumping, her panicking heart, her blouse soaked through where she splashed and sweated. She dared not look at her reflection: the eyes that say *I can*. I did. The murderer in the glass.

1

On Thursday, two weeks after posting his letter to Joseph Gribble and having no reply, Mr Wye took the train into London, briefcase in hand, to knock personally at the door. It was an extraordinary measure, to go so far – one and a half hours on the train – particularly for a man of his age. Five years retired but still in his office every weekday, Mr Wye had made that particular journey for many years. He took pleasure in waking early, plenty of time for toast with marmalade and a cup of tea, then off to the station where he parked his little car. Once on board, he took another cup of tea from a vendor passing through and read *The Times* from cover to cover. Then, with time to spare before his arrival at Paddington, he quietly observed his travelling companions.

There were the usual businessmen keeping busy with mobile phones and laptop computers (in Mr Wye's glory days, he carried not one but two leather briefcases, in which he transported his paperwork). Behind him sat two young women, overdressed, eyes like piss-holes in the snow. They chewed gum. 'Then she calls and says to him, "I want to see you." Right? She's in town. She looks like the back end of a bus now. Remember her at school? Queen bee! She thought she was queen bee. She ain't queen bee no more. He says to me that he don't want her, but I know he's texting.'

'Oh, he never.'

'He is!' There was a pause. 'I want a nose job.'

'What's wrong with your nose?'

'It's too big. My dad says it looks like a potato. And see this bump on my chin? That's a wart starting. I want it gone.'

'I want my boobs done. There's a guy, a registered doctor, who does it for eight hundred.'

'I'm prettier than her, right?'

'He ain't worth it.'

Watching them from across the aisle was a boy of about seventeen, already a hard man, red-faced with unspent steam, the kind with a passion for fighting, with a life in which everything tested his power. A boil simmered on his neck. The boy spread his legs and thudded his trainers to some driving internal rhythm – techno beats – but they ignored him strenuously.

The table a bit further along was filled with students – they became drama students as the journey went on, reciting aloud to one another, their voices increasingly strident. Someone said, 'What a lot of show-offs.' Now they had an audience. The speeches continued the rest of the way to London. Mr Wye sighed. It was too tedious.

The train arrived on time, much to his satisfaction. Stepping from the carriage, he blundered for a moment:

Paddington was not the same. A shopping mall lay before him, a vulgar emporium, lit up like Christmas. He stood and stared until the crowd carried him along, charged from every side as if he weren't there. Where was his briefcase? Still in hand. And his wallet? The angry boy on the train – he'd got it. The boy had picked it off him.

No, here it was, in his jacket pocket.

He patted himself, repeated the mantra: spectacles, testicles, wallet and watch. After a visit to the Gents, where he paid thirty pence and called it daylight robbery under his breath, he joined the taxi rank.

He was in and out of taxis all day, going from house to house. He kept receipts. He was, after all, visiting on behalf of the family. The houses he saw were, for the most part, in a state of dereliction. Their inhabitants were old women – he had a list of their names. In two houses there were vagrants, delinquents, ragged young people, clearly out of work, claiming they were artists and suchlike. He ordered them to vacate the premises at once. He had the law behind him, he said. For the most part, he was treated with respect. The women remembered him and he ticked off their names one by one. The dead ones, or presumed dead, with squatters living in their houses, using their things – picking up where they left off – he crossed out.

The house in the Crescent, once as familiar to him as his own home, was his last stop of the day. As with the other houses on his list, it was a right mess. Sagging, shedding stucco, begrimed, bashed on all sides, bald of paint; great curls of it had dropped off since he'd last been, which was years ago – how many years? Five or six, at least. All around, other houses had been gutted, flayed, done up in white throughout, white as bone, with the corpse flesh stripped away: a house as fresh as an egg, the bog replaced with a tidy garden shed in which to keep the tools, the paint. So too would this house soon have that fate.

Mr Wye rang the bell. A few minutes passed. He rang again, longer, harder. He had seen two women sitting in the window. He knocked. It was his knock they answered.

*

Rita was drinking a cup of tea. They had their chairs pulled up to the front window of the drawing room, she and Annetta, watching the street through the grey mist of net curtains. Not saying much, for, as Rita often thought, what was there to say to a person who had lost her mind? Joseph was out. Days had passed since Annetta's most recent escape and he had been especially vigilant, cooped up in the house, hardly daring to sleep at night. Shadows under his eyes. Rita had sent him off to ride the buses for a while. That's what he liked. The fresh air would do him good.

'Well. Look who it is,' Rita said.

'What?'

'Here he is again, the bastard. I can't believe my eyes.'

'Who's that?' Annetta said. 'I've never seen that man before in my life.'

'Sure you have. It's *him*.'

'Who?'

'What's-his-name. Wye. That one.'

'What?'

'Mr Wye. *You* know. Gillies' man.'

And Annetta replied, with a certain lucidity, 'Is it, now? I thought he was dead. Why did I think that?'

'I wish he was,' Rita grumbled. 'Nothing but trouble. Probably looking for another freebie, if I know the man. And I *know* the man.'

He had a knock that made them jump: *rat-a-tat-tat*. 'Ought we to answer it?' Annetta said.

'I reckon he's seen us sitting here.' Neither one moved.

'If we stay perfectly still, maybe he'll go away,' Annetta whispered.

He knocked again. Rita stood. 'You stay here.' But Annetta kept close, holding onto her skirt.

'What do you want?' Rita said from behind the door.

'I'd like to come in, please.'

Rita hesitated.

'Shall I call for assistance? I see a policeman across the way in the park,' Mr Wye said.

Rita opened the door. He hadn't changed – aged, as they all were, still with a thick head of hair, gone silver now, and wearing his usual black suit and tie. Rita could smell him from across the threshold. He was the kind that kept scrupulously clean, she remembered, bathing after every exertion, and he smelled of soap and talcum powder and hair lotion. His underwear had been rough and white with bleach, pressed for him by his wife, not that she was to mention his wife – that would be profane. His wife, she gathered, was a saint, as devout as they came here on earth.

'You again,' Rita said.

'I sent a letter to Joseph Gribble, to which I've had no reply. Am I right to assume he still lives at this address?'

'It's none of your business.'

Mr Wye cleared his throat. 'It is my business.'

Annetta, who had been standing behind Rita the whole time, suddenly bent double and howled, pointing at Mr Wye. 'You know,' she said through tears. 'You know. You know what you did.'

He flushed, despite himself. 'I'm afraid I don't know.'

'You're a devil,' Annetta cried, dropping to her knees. She tore at her clothes and ground her teeth.

'Go on,' Rita said, nudging her with one foot. 'Off you go.' Annetta crawled back into the drawing room – they heard her after she disappeared, the metallic scrape of her anguish, as if it bit her on the inside.

'We're still here, as you can see,' Rita said to Mr Wye, and she shut the door with a bang.

2

Mr Wye was gone, but the taint of him remained. His smell – it had got into the house. Unsettling, to see that man again. It drew her nerves tight; she was trembling. Oh, she wouldn't let it show, but the feeling was there all the same: the fear of him, from long ago. Annetta's head lay in Rita's lap. Rita did her best to soothe her but after a while she was fed up and put Annetta to bed, locking the door, the key in her pocket.

She stood there for a minute and heard Annetta get up and rattle the knob, calling for freedom. Rita could stand it. Better in than out, she always said – or was it the other way round?

Further along the corridor was where Joseph slept, but she never bothered going in, knowing the room to be a solid mess of old newspapers, bus schedules and sweet wrappers, everywhere growing mould, the cups of tea and old sand-wiches and whatnot, and his clothes all over the floor in nasty piles that he kicked about, finding them in his way. If that's how he chose to live – *well*. The bathroom was the same: pure filth, although it had been a temple once, walled in marble, with his-and-hers sinks and a shower that sprayed from all sides and spewed steam. Nothing worked now, except the toilet. Joseph could never be bothered to flush it himself. Rita turned away – then went back, holding her nose, and flushed.

Down a flight of stairs, for Joseph and Annetta were on the second floor, where Rita paused outside the door to the room that had once been hers. No one had slept there since she left the house, although the furniture and all the pictures and fittings remained – golden everything, still resplendent, the whole room draped in damask that was tied up here and there in fat ropes of silk braid. A glittering, faceted tent, when candles were lit, utterly dramatic. The bed was made; it had been made for twenty years. She never wanted to sleep in that bed again.

Sal's room was next, untouched since her death, fit for a queen, grander even than Rita's parlour, in desperate crimson. More encrusted, wreathed, swagged and gilded – and for all its luxurious trappings, serene. A sense of Sal, the woman she had been. Joseph liked to look at his mother's things, the many fine gifts she had been given in her lifetime, the valuable trinkets, carved intricacies, enamel, needlework, jewels in boxes, couture dresses in plastic. When Rita caught him mooning there, wiping away the tears, she shooed him out of the room: it didn't do to dwell, she told him.

Rita went downstairs and curled up on the old chesterfield to wait for Joseph's return. She smelled the dust; it puffed as she turned this way, then that. She sat up straight – she stood, jumped to her feet as if she had rubber bands in her knees. Rita was bothered. She went to the window, looking for Joseph, anxious for him to come back so she could be on her way to her flat in Camden. Mr Wye had spooked her.

He had been a regular visitor once upon a time. When Sal was still alive and he came round, he would always stay for a cup of tea, sneaking looks at Sal when he thought she wasn't looking. He was gone on her – always had been. Her shoulders drooped with relief when he left, although she never spoke a word against him. If Sal despised Mr Wye as Rita and Annetta did, she never said. The way he looked at Sal, besotted with unsatisfied love – *well*. It turned Rita's stomach. Sal was only sweet to him to keep her house, Mr Wye being Arthur Gillies' main henchman and most trusted employee, his eyes and ears; a nasty bird, the ace of spades, a buzzard bringing death.

After a long time of watching at the window, Rita had to sit or her legs would give. She stretched out on the chesterfield again and, despite herself, let her eyes close. She slept at once and her dreams were strange. She dreamed of home – it was a recurring dream. She saw another version of her life inside the shabby rooms of the house in which she had been born and where, perhaps, her family still lived. She saw the life she would have known among the people who always said they knew her best; the person she would have become under their watch. Rita on the night shift at the chemical factory, listening to the machines hiss and slam.

Rita in a kitchen that smelled of cat piss, handing out greasy cups. Walls marbled with grime, children unwashed, hopping with bugs. Rita down the pub, drunk as they come, led by a gang of young men to an abandoned house. Rita from Widnes, not London. *That* Rita.

She was trouble from the start, so people said, and once puberty hit, her boldness came out in a blaze. Too good-looking, that was always her problem, and a man-eater to boot. The whole town talked, and how! She would wake to a noisy dawn chorus, the bickering begun, in sweet voices, over a worm. When she left the house, rooks hooked for her eyes and the bits of gold she wore in her ears. Fat geese lined up like a row of justices at the front gate. Wherever she walked, pigeons shat, squirts of chalk that spattered her shoes, and gulls from the Mersey dived at her head, unpicking her careful curls. Her mother, a threadbare chicken, caught her out in the kitchen while she ate her bread and dripping. 'It will kill him,' she whispered, meaning Rita's father. She battered Rita, slapped her, the tales she'd heard chopped up and stuck back together all wrong. No one cared what Rita heard said about her, whether it was true or not. It was generally felt that she deserved to hear those cruel remarks: a girl so beautiful they wanted to tear her apart. She stalked Widnes in a yellow dress and high heels, lipsticked ear to ear, and the birds followed her everywhere.

When Rita married, aged seventeen, there was a stunned silence. And then, the great hypocrisy: the wings of the community drawing round her. The luck of that Rita, they said, to find a man who would have her for good. A baby would put her right now. Oh yes, a baby.

He was a stranger, a sailor ashore who found his way inland to the chemical factory and got caught up in town life. He spent enough time in the pubs to become known to Rita's father and brothers, and so he was brought home and presented to her late one night. Men in the kitchen, swaying on their feet, a blur of faces and mended shirts, and Rita, who had been drinking Blue Nun with her mother when they all trooped through the door; Rita in a puddle of light. The stranger, laughing, unshaven, missing his molars, was shoved forward. They met. He took her hand, pulled her to her feet. There were whistles, clapping. Her mother hissed something Rita didn't quite catch and her father slapped her mother and told her to shut it. Rita didn't have to look at her father to know how fearsome he was: his misshapen face streaked with burns, caustic splashes; eyes squeezed into slits, a cauliflower ear.

The sailor drew her into the hall and kissed her. He threw his hand up her skirt, straight into her knickers. She rocked against him and he was solid. They went out back, past the bog, into the field where the ragwort flourished, and they did it right there with the moon hiding in the trees.

It went on like that for a few weeks, hot and fast, and they soon announced they would marry. It was plain to see they were in love, always together except for shifts, down the pub or in bed, the sailor having his own bedsit – she had already moved in with him. Rita wanted a party, and didn't she get drunk and kiss every man she danced with and let them stuff notes into her brassiere? She could hardly stand up at the end of the night, and neither could anyone else, either.

In bed, her new husband wanted to show her things. 'I'm a citizen of the world. I'm telling you this because I'm telling you what I need. You're hot as hell. You got the right ideas.' She'd kept herself clean, he said, putting his nose in. 'You have a nice thing down there. That's what I need. That's *all* I need, and plenty of it.' He kissed her everywhere – she thought she would die of pleasure. 'You're pretty. Whores ain't pretty, and you ain't really a whore, no matter what people say.'

'Is that what they say?' Rita tossed her head.

'I want a wife now. You better listen to me.'

She laughed. 'Then tell me what it is I'm to be doing.'

'That's right. It's my rules now,' he said.

She was curious about whores and asked him all about them as they rested together after. Whoring, he said, was something young girls were talked into by older men. 'Sometimes they're so young and thick they can't do any-thing else in this world. There's some that have had plain bad luck and you know they won't get far. But there's some girls that do it because they want to. They can't think about any-thing else. Everything to them is sex. I met one or two of them and they were something special. That's the kind of girl I'm always looking for.'

'I'm your girl. You know I am.'

'There's some that *live* it.'

'I live it. I been living it for years.' Rita gazed at him, loving him, wanting him to believe her.

But he didn't seem to hear; he was remembering. 'The young girls, the virgins, they cost dear at first, but there's a lot of yelling with them. It ain't worth it, when you think you're hurting someone. Then there's your two-bit whore and she's an old girl, an old horse, knackered and done for.'

There were the poor dark girls in foreign ports lying motionless under a white man, and the English workhorses with their barnacled calves and breasts like long-drawn udders: the scrubbers. There were the drinkers falling into a ditch, taking a man down with them, and always there was the queue of sailors and soldiers tailing back, waiting their turn. She knew it should fill her with horror, to hear him talk so. Why didn't it fill her with horror?

She wanted him to come to her like he was paying for it. She wanted to feel the difference – she, who had never made anyone pay to have his way with her. She asked him to wait outside the door and knock. He had to show her his money and put it on the dresser before she lay back and did what he told her.

It seemed a good enough marriage. She didn't think much about it at the time. She was happy, she would have said.

The first night he didn't come home, Rita's thighs were aching. There was supper on the table, for she'd hurried back from old Mrs Benson's, where she did housekeeping, to cook and change her dress. The supper sat, Rita with it, waiting for the pubs to close. Gone midnight, he was still not home, nor had he returned when the milk float rattled past. At dawn she locked the door to their bedsit. She knew

– of course she knew. She took the day off sick from Mrs Benson's and prowled Widnes, just to be sure, a house sparrow chirruping over her shoulder. Then she went home and tidied up and made his tea as usual and when he finally returned that evening, she didn't say, 'Where you been?' She knew. There was a girl named Diane, a young war widow who looked as if she could do no harm but who only liked married men.

Rita said, 'Here you are, my love,' and set down a plate of sausages and mash. He ate, not looking at her, pushing his plate away when he was done. He wiped his mouth on his sleeve, stood up and made to leave. She couldn't stop herself from asking, 'Will you be back tonight?' and heard the words break apart in her mouth. He didn't answer, already out of the door, and then she was at the window, watching him go.

He mostly stayed away after that. Sometimes he stopped home in the morning for a bit of breakfast before work and sometimes he was gone for days at a stretch and his shirt was a new one when he reappeared, wanting tea and comfort. Rita sat each evening and waited for him. She prepared a meal – she couldn't eat a bite herself but studied each plateful, looking for her mistakes. Her potatoes turned to powder. Her cod smelt rank. There was fat in the gravy. He didn't eat greens. The milk was off again. Her meat pie was underdone except where it had burned on top, and didn't she cry over that pie while he stared at her? Wasn't he raging hungry after a shift at the chemical plant, and didn't he hate to see a girl cry? She had let him see her with her face unmade-up, wearing the raggedy brassiere that was most comfortable under her housecoat. She had told him everything about herself; she had talked all night sometimes, pressing him about his life: she wanted to be close to him. He didn't want to be close. He didn't want a housewife, a maker of gravy and meat pies, a woman who cried over the cooking. He wanted a whore.

He was leaving anyway, going back to sea. That's what he told her when she threw herself at his feet. Married life didn't suit him after all. He would collect his next pay and be gone. Then he led her to bed. He rode her raw and she stuffed her fingers into her mouth to stop from crying out. After it was done, she waited for him to sleep, then Rita picked his pocket and fled into the night.

No one was surprised to hear she had caught a ride to London. Hadn't she been carrying on the last month of her marriage with a bus conductor? Or was it a train driver? Whoever he was, he was a man with wheels.

That was the birds again, putting her story to the wind.

*

He drove a taxi. His name was Paul, although that didn't matter for she never saw him after. A quickie in the back seat and he was off, having deposited Rita outside a guesthouse in Ladbroke Grove where he thought she might stay. He lived round the corner with his wife and children. Just round the corner, he said. It would be easy enough to get to her. She smiled and nodded. She had smiled so much;

laughed and chatted, all the way from Widnes to London. That's what a girl did when she wanted something.

Rita stood at the door of the guesthouse and pretended to knock until he'd driven off in search of fares. Then she walked. Her fever carried her along – it was like being ill, taking the first steps in the direction of Soho. She knew what it meant. Fast girls went to Soho. Tarts. The women running the tills of the shops where Rita stopped to ask the way turned their backs on her. Birds, all of them, bitchy old crows.

The evening drew in and the lamps of the city were lit inside and out. London was still a shambles; there was work for a brickie, work for a sparks, but she couldn't be a brickie or a sparks. She took a drink at a pub, stopped a few more times, celebrating the sights, spending her last pennies on Blue Nun. She saw Kensington Park and Marble Arch. She heard a man declaim from Speaker's Corner, a burning candle in his hand. She picked up Oxford Street, marvelling at the department store windows, brilliantly dressed, advertising all sorts, then turned down Regent Street and followed its curve.

It was late when she finally reached Soho: half wrecked or half built, buzzing with exotic life such as she had never seen; people everywhere, more people than ever at that hour, women in all kinds of get-up, rattling bunches of keys to draw attention, and the punters that surrounded them just as raucous. She found a room easily enough at the YWCA and slept on a hard camp bed in a full dormitory. The next day, on the advice of the girl who served her breakfast, she took a job doing coat check in the Colony Room. If she were willing to work at night, she would always find employment. 'It's the day jobs that are scarce. I'd like to be a typist,' the girl had said.

'Who wouldn't?' another said, zooming past with a tray of toast. 'Not on your feet all day – that's the life.'

Rita dressed for the Colony Room with care, showing her long white neck and regal shoulders, her tiny waist accentuated by a full skirt under which anything might happen. She loved to watch the rich folks swinging by, dragging their furs. They whirled around the room in glamorous pairs, laughing as if they didn't have a care in the world. She longed to be out on the dance floor. She danced a bit herself among the coats, wrapping their sleeves around her. Sometimes she slipped off to the broom cupboard with a bloke – a nice little earner. She made enough to get her own bedsit, but London was always showing her what could be hers, if she only had the money.

'Let me sell cigarettes,' Rita said to the manager.

'I ain't seen more than your legs yet,' he replied, but even when he'd seen the whole of her, he kept her in the cloakroom – he kept her for himself.

She worked all hours, until the place shut up for the night and everyone stumbled home with the sun in their eyes. When she'd had enough of checking coats, she moved on to one of the new Gaggia milk bars, thinking it would be a modern experience, there among the potted plants. The milk bar was full of clean-cut young men who called her 'doll' and told her, when they took her out for a drink, that they wanted to respect her. She laughed, excused herself to powder her nose and slipped away. There was no money in what they wanted.

She took a job as a chambermaid in a five-star hotel. She studied the way the hotel guests slept in their beds, the contents of their bins, the state of the bathroom – she looked boldly into the toilet bowl and marvelled at what came off on the brush, what had been flushed: till receipts, a man's wallet, a black lace brassiere with holes cut out. She sifted the dregs of their cups; she could read tea leaves and so she knew their futures, whoever they were, wherever. Nothing put her off. She slept with the hotel manager every morning on his break and he added ten hours to her time card each week.

Then she wanted to be on the stage, so she made her way to the Windmill. She heard they were always looking for girls. 'Proper English girls. I'm an English rose. That's what they want. Just look at my colouring,' said the girl at the front of the queue. 'I'm a trained ballerina.'

'I'm good on roller skates,' another girl said.

'I can do the scarf dance.'

'I can pony-trot.'

'I can tap-dance.'

Rita kept quiet. She knew what she was good at, too.

'What I want is a touring variety show,' one girl said. 'I want to see the world. They pay for your travel and board. All you got to do is stand onstage a few hours every night.'

'You take your clothes off, too, you big dummy. That's the show.'

The girl behind nudged Rita. 'What about you? I'm from Leicester. I came down on the bus two days ago. My mum don't know where I am – she thinks I'm looking after my sister's new baby. How about that for a joke?'

When the stage door was unlocked, they all pushed in at once. They were shown where they could undress: a corridor where the buckets and brooms were kept. 'Just down to your knickers and bra for the first pass.' One by one the girls filed past several men, all wearing suits and sucking on cigarettes. Waiting her turn, Rita smelled the room, the choking smoke, the soured floorboards and body odour. There wasn't a window – there wasn't a sun in there.

When it was her turn, she didn't get far. 'Come on, darling, blondes only.' She started to dance. 'I don't want to see you shimmy. I want blondes. Who's next?' So Rita went across the road to the peepshow and was hired on the spot.

She had to be with the boss of the Cul de Sac and then she had to be with his friends, but Rita wasn't getting paid extra, although she suspected the boss was. When she complained, he said, 'If you don't like it, there's another girl out there to take your place. Girls like you are a dime a dozen.'

Rita shut up. She put out. She went to him when he called her name – the boss called her Margarita. In that godforsaken room, his office in the eaves, she tried to think of other things. She listened to the pigeons cooing, a big family of them perched on the window ledge. His elbow at the back of her neck. He had bad breath. His teeth were chipped like an old mug. He wheezed and heaved – he smoked cigars continuously and the hair that thickly covered him made her itch.

A seagull screamed – so far from the Mersey. A seagull in the middle of Soho, down a greasy alley, in a cranny: a *seagull*. Another one, and then many, until there were hundreds of them, from the sound of it. They drew in like a storm cloud and chased off the pigeons. They covered the roof, squawking and fighting, pummelling wings; chinks of light appeared in the ceiling like stars where the tiles dislodged. More came, rubbish spilling from their beaks: the bits they picked up from the street, sandwich crusts and snips of string, butcher's paper, newsprint, potato skins. The noise was incredible. Rita shook her head. The boss gave her a slap. He was done.

She rolled to the floor and found her clothes and shoes. Shaking, she made her way down the narrow, turning stairs to a dressing room full of half-naked girls. She took her place before the mirrors. She blew her nose and powdered her face, fluffed her curls. She drew on eyebrows and a mouth. A bell rang. Rita walked down a corridor. She stepped inside a cupboard that had a curtain down the middle and a single chair, separated from her by some glass. Nine hours passed.

There were certain women who frequented the peepshow, making no secret of why they were there. Some of them were butch, but others were more maternal: stocky, soft-looking women, soberly dressed. Nell was one of those mothers, well known around Soho, and once she saw Rita she carried on a crush for months, stopping by every afternoon, tapping on the glass. She always had a favourite to whom she was devoted, but she was fickle, too. Rita waited for it to pass. Nell sat with her legs open, skirt hitched above her knees. *Transfixed*. But Rita was no ingénue. She knew all about Nell, how she liked the young girls and hunted them down, targeting the ones she called green. She was kind to them, bought them meals if they were hungry, clothes if they needed them, and let them stay in her room above the Sugar Shop, most of them having nowhere else to sleep. It was there that she taught them to please her.

'Fancy a cuppa?'

Rita always said no. 'I'm not that kind of girl,' she told Nell.

Nell laughed. 'What kind do you mean?'

Rita looked Nell straight in the eye. 'Your kind.'

'It's just a cup of tea, darling. Nothing to be frightened of.'

'I'm not scared of you,' Rita had answered, but she was, a bit. She was curious, too. She'd heard from other girls about long nights of petting, of pleasures exclusively female. Initiation, they called it. Some said it was pure love, what happened between women.

As usual, Nell was waiting outside the Cul de Sac when Rita finished her shift. Rita, with the hectoring voices of seagulls still in her head, finally said yes. She only wanted someone to be nice to her. Off they went to Lyons where, despite the crowd and queues, Nell found them a booth in the Grill & Cheese. The servers knew Nell, and the cooks did, too. Tea appeared unbidden, and sandwiches and wedges of cake, cheese and biscuits, a plate of fresh fruit polished to a shine.

'You're skin and bones,' Nell said. 'Not an ounce of fat on you. I like a girl with something to hold onto. Most folks do.'

'Even if I ate a steak every day, it wouldn't stick to me,' Rita said.

'You weren't so thin as this when I first saw you. You're not taking care of yourself. What are you earning a week? Twenty pound? Twenty-five?'

'I got everyone asking for me.' If Rita didn't eat because she wanted a new dress, it was nobody's business but her own.

Then they needed a drink. Nell said she had a bottle and that sounded good to Rita so they moved on to Nell's room above the Sugar Shop, where they sat back against a pile of cushions on the bed. Rita was wary, but only just, and she was soon disarmed, for the whisky warmed her through and Nell was a laugh, even if her hands did wander. Once Nell started on stories there was no stopping her. She reminded Rita of the sailor, with her talk of whores.

It was after midnight. They had been together for hours and finished their bottle. No, Rita said when Nell went under her skirt. Stop. Please. Rita pushed Nell away at last, a great shove that knocked the wind out of her.

Nell got to her feet. Sturdy and strong, she stood like a man, her softness gone. 'You think you know a thing or two, but you're only a filly. You need me.'

'I can look after myself, thank you.' Rita tried to stand but Nell pushed her down on the bed.

'We'd make a great team, you and me. We could make money. Girls who look like you make money, but you got to manage it a certain way. I know how. I want my own place, my own show, and I need a star. You're my star. You've got sex appeal. Everyone says so.'

Rita looked past Nell to the door. She had thought nothing of it when Nell locked up, but where had the key gone? 'It's time I went home,' she said.

Nell reached for Rita's hand, her voice wheedling now. 'Come on, let's dance. Do you hear the music coming up from downstairs? It's loud enough – let's dance to it.'

'I don't want to dance.'

'Let's dance,' Nell insisted, pulling Rita to her feet. 'Have another drink, dance with me, let me love you. I want to be with you. If you were mine, I could do anything, I tell you.'

'How many times do I have to say it?' Rita pulled clear. Nell's eyes were full of tears but nothing could make Rita love Nell the way she wanted her to. Nell unlocked the door.

'Rita,' Nell called after her when she was halfway down the stairs.

Despite herself, Rita turned back – Nell lunged, kissed her. Rita wanted to spit. Nell saw the look on her face and let her go.

*

Nell had to have her. She pestered Rita at the Cul de Sac; she sat in her booth, feeding the meter, and Rita gyrated while Nell wept. Nell begged and bullied, she boasted – she assured Rita she was already in love with another woman even as she gazed at Rita for hours on end. Rita held her nerve. When Nell waited for her after work, she shook her head. Nell followed her home and sometimes she was outside in the morning when Rita emerged from her bedsit. Sometimes she was too drunk to stand. Weeks passed like that. The boss was fed up. He said Nell scared off the customers.

It was a relief when, finally, one day Nell did not appear – nor, for that matter, did anyone else. Traffic to Rita's window at the peepshow slowed almost to a stop, without even faithful Nell to drop coins into the box. Rita lost her job. What's more, when she looked for work, there was none to be found, not in Soho at least. She had a feeling it was something to do with Nell. She went to Nell's room above the Sugar Shop and found it empty, except for the bed, which had been broken into pieces. No one seemed to know anything about Nell. They all knew who Rita was. She didn't have to say her name or why she wanted Nell. They knew. The birds had seen to that – the pigeons and seagulls.

To spite them, Rita stayed in Soho. It was just like her to do so. She had some money put aside, enough to keep her going for a short time. Rita didn't retreat, although she kept to herself. By day she saw the sights of London and at night she stayed indoors with the blackout shades drawn. Just like during the war. She might get a bottle of something to pass the hours, but she couldn't afford the habit. A bottle of sweet sherry, nothing dear – she'd acquired a taste for it at the Colony Room.

She ran through her money soon enough and had to quit her bedsit. So it was, packing up her things, not sure what she would do next, that Rita found, among the postcards and ticket stubs and burst-off buttons she hadn't needle and thread for, a card that a gentleman had slipped her, the coat-check girl. No telephone number, just an address and the name of the woman who lived there. 'She'll look after you,' Arthur Gillies said. Having seen him at the Colony Room many times, Rita knew well who he was. Arthur Gillies was all pop-eyes and no-colour mouth, his suits beautifully made to hide his fat. She had offered him the broom cupboard. He refused, but his eyes never left hers.

He might remember her. Rita put his card in her purse. Her bits and pieces were packed in a box tied with string. She needed a cup of tea – there was just enough in her pocket for Lyons. She passed the Sugar Shop on the way. The room was empty the last time she looked, but you never knew with Nell.

Sure enough, the key under the mat was gone. Rita tried the door: locked. She knocked. 'Nell? Are you there, Nell? It's me.' She listened. Someone was there. She could hear breathing catching on itself, then nothing. The breath held. She knocked again: shave and a haircut, six bits. 'Nell?'

'There's no Nell here.' Not exactly Nell's voice, but close.

'Oh, come on, Nell. It's me. Rita. From the Cul de Sac.'

'Who?'

'Rita.' She kept her tone light. 'They said you got married. They said you were dead. Someone said you turned up on a building site with a brick in your head. How about that? I knew you couldn't be dead, Nell. Not you.'

'What do you want?'

'Only to say hello. I was on my way to Lyons.'

'Anyone with you?'

'Just me.'

'How do I know?'

'Open the door, Nell. I've had enough of this now.'

She heard furniture moving and the lock undone. The door opened: a girl, younger and smaller than Rita, who was herself only eighteen. Her fair hair – piles of it – was tied back, showing how pale and underfed she was, her eyes red-rimmed. 'I'm not Nell, as you can see, but for God's sake come in.'

Rita stepped inside and the girl slammed the door, locking it with trembling fingers.

'Have you got trouble?' Rita said.

'What do you know? Who are you? I never seen you before in my life.'

'I'm a friend of Nell's.'

'What kind of friend?'

Rita laughed. 'Just a friend. But I haven't seen her around.'

'I don't know where she is.'

'Has she been gone long?' Rita said. The girl didn't reply. 'Did she say where she was going?'

'She's not here. There was nothing here. Just the bed, and that was in pieces, but I managed to mend it well enough.'

The bed had been moved across the room from where it

was before and now stood next to the door. 'One of life's necessities,' Rita said, patting the bed. 'I know this old rocking horse, don't I?'

The girl looked at her. 'I suppose you do.'

'I'm not like that,' Rita said quickly. 'I only meant—'

'You better go now.'

'I haven't got anywhere to go, have I? Nell's seen to that.'

'I don't know,' the girl said, looking away.

'Don't know what?'

'About Nell.' The girl began to cry.

'It wasn't like that between me and Nell.'

'Like what?'

'I don't love her, if that's what you're asking.'

'I'm so lonely without her,' the girl wailed.

'I could stay. Just for a cup of tea, if you're having one. I could do with a cup of tea myself – I was on my way to Lyons when I stopped.'

The girl shuffled her feet, bare as they were, cold-looking, made of shrivelled skin and swollen joints, the toes shrunken, missing nails. Not pretty feet. She saw Rita looking at them. 'Trench foot,' she said.

Rita helped her push the bed into place. She wanted it against the door. Then Rita put the kettle on and they sat down together on the floor.

*

At first Annetta shook and was sick – that was the tablets mucking about with her system, Rita said.

'He'll be back,' Annetta fretted.

'Of course he will,' Rita said. 'But we'll be ready for him.'

He was Sylvain, Annetta's ponce. She said he was her boyfriend. Rita knew him from the Cul de Sac. He supplied a few of the girls who worked there and he was always trying to get into the dressing room. Annetta wanted to break with him – she swore she did – but he carried on coming round all hours that first night, sometimes with other men in tow, and they banged on the door as if they would break it down. Rita shouted that she would call the police. Even with the door locked and the bed there and Rita standing guard, Annetta trembled. Rita thought she might go out of the window. She boiled the kettle and brewed endless pots of tea to give them strength and keep them awake. Eventually Sylvain went away, but they didn't dare sleep.

In the morning, Rita slipped out and bought what they needed – milk, bread, butter, eggs, for Annetta looked half starved. They passed a second night, and then a third, in the room above the Sugar Shop, Rita nursing Annetta, making her eat and drink. There was no sign of Nell, but Sylvain was always at the door. The door wouldn't take much more – the hinges looked about to pop from the way he hammered. Rita knew they had to get out of there.

'Have a look at this,' she said, producing the card from her purse. 'Have you heard of Arthur Gillies?'

'Who's he?'

'He's a big shot,' Rita said. 'He's got houses.'

'I don't know what you're on about.'

'He runs a closed-door business. It's all safe and clean.

Should be good money, if he'll have us. When you've fattened up a bit. He don't take just anyone, you know. He's choosy – it's the crème de la crème he's after. We're good-looking. You're so delicate and pretty, a proper dolly bird, and I'm dark, and he'll like the contrast, the way we set each other off.'

'Do you really think we stand a chance?'

'I think it's the only chance we got.'

'Arthur Gillies might have you but he won't take me. I'm not high-class enough.'

'Sure, we're a double act, aren't we? I won't do it without you. You're the only friend I've got.'

Annetta gulped at the Scotch broth Rita had fetched up. When she had drunk it all, she asked for more.

'That's my girl,' said Rita.

*

Arthur Gillies specialized in privacy. He didn't advertise – he didn't need to. He owned many houses and each one had its madam, happy in her status, running the girls and keeping the books. Every man who walked through the door was vetted in some way, his position verified, his ancestry traced. Half the time a girl didn't know the real name of the man she was with, even if she recognized his face – she was expected to conceal her excitement with a film star, to grin and bear it with the aristocrats who barked and smelled of dogs.

Looking at the house in the Crescent, one would never

think of what went on inside. It was grand enough, standing four storeys tall, its stucco just-minted in white gloss, the door brass on fire, window boxes overflowing their bounty. A rose climbed, filling the air with fragrance.

Rita marched up to the front door and rang the bell; Annetta lagged. 'Smile,' Rita urged. Annetta showed her teeth. Rita wanted to pinch her. She'd had a time of it getting Annetta to leave the room above the Sugar Shop. Annetta was deathly pale under her rouge and she bit at her lipstick. All the way there, Rita had kept firm hold of her, feeling how she shook: like a train ran through her!

The woman who answered the door was smartly dressed, nothing in her manner to suggest she was an outlaw. She greeted them cordially and invited them in – she seemed to understand the purpose of their visit. She led them to a double front room, which she called the drawing room. Rita had never been in a drawing room before. 'Please sit down,' the woman said, indicating two armchairs upholstered in horsehair. She took her place by the mantelpiece, where she stood, erect, bejewelled, beautifully coiffed, a sleek black cap of hair fitted closely to her head in a sharp bob, not a strand out of place.

'Nice room,' Rita said, glancing round.

'I haven't introduced myself. I'm Sal and this is my house.' Sal was the name on the card in Rita's possession, the name she had memorized. Sal Gribble. It wasn't much of a name, to Rita's mind, but the woman herself was a stunner. Sal studied them from on high. Annetta slithered down the horsehair chair – her feet didn't even touch the ground when she sat, so little was she, and the slippery haircloth slid her right off onto the floor until she gripped the sides of the chair and held on.

Sal said, 'You might as well know, I don't take pairs. Too much trouble. Lovers' spats and all.'

Rita said, 'It ain't like that.'

'*Isn't*,' Sal corrected. 'We speak the Queen's English here.'

'We isn't,' Rita said. Annetta flushed.

Sal gave Rita a hard stare and put out her hand. 'It was a pleasure meeting you.'

'Pardon?'

'I'll show you to the door.'

'Please,' Annetta said. 'Don't listen to her – she doesn't know what she's saying.'

But Rita was on her feet, eyes ablaze. 'I don't stand for disrespect. I am a perfectly decent person.'

'I don't have room for troublemakers,' Sal said.

'What is it with you? Calling people names. Arthur Gillies personally gave me this card. I have met Arthur Gillies.'

'Arthur Gillies, you say? Arthur Gillies indeed. You certainly make a lot of noise and *Arthur Gillies* does not like noise.'

'Oh,' said Annetta, standing between them, wringing her hands.

At that moment Arthur Gillies walked through the door. Rita nudged Annetta, who curtsied.

'What's going on here?' he said, addressing Sal.

'They're not staying,' she replied. 'They were just leaving.'

Arthur Gillies looked at them, at Rita, his eyes lingering.

35

He nodded, liking what he saw. He didn't look at Sal, but took hold of Annetta's hand and shook it hard, then did the same with Rita. He had hands like frying pans. Annetta's hand liquefied in his, but Rita returned the shake.

'What's your name?' he asked her.

'I'm Rita. And this is Annette.'

'Annetta,' she whispered.

'That's right,' Rita said.

'Welcome,' said Arthur Gillies. 'I hope you'll be happy here.'

And they were. For a good long while, at least.

3

He thought he'd like to punch the door. He didn't dare, but the instinct was there, always the instinct was there. Mr Wye wouldn't be treated that way, not by those women. He spoke to the door. 'You're nothing. I could turf you out if I wanted to.'

A movement from the window drew his attention: Rita's face, the *no* of it. She'd always been trouble. He knew she liked a drink. You could see it in the ruddy sag of her cheeks, the pouched eyes, dead set, full of red; the fireworks of burst capillaries. Arthur Gillies had ordered her from the house more than once but he always took her back, like a fool. Certain women got to him and she was one of them, although Mr Wye couldn't see it himself. She was good-looking, but not like Sal.

He had never been with Sal. He'd been with nearly every other girl that worked for Arthur Gillies – they were on the house, Gillies said, and Mr Wye took full advantage of the offer. But not Sal. When Gillies fell for a girl, he fell hard, and he never fell as hard for a girl as he did for Sal. Sal was the making of him. She turned him famous just by being herself: London's own Bettie Page.

Once Sal had borne Joseph, she was untouchable. Gillies wouldn't admit the boy was his, but everyone knew. Joseph was the spit of him.

Mr Wye had no children. It might have all turned out differently if he had, not that he had regrets. He'd lived a noble life. He'd worked hard. He did not aspire to the leisure of retirement, long days of television, bowling on the green, hot tea in hot weather – how refreshing. He gave to the church, even though it was unfashionable to do so these days, and when his wife died he paid for a whole new pew in her name, right at the front, with a long buttoned cushion in burgundy velvet. She had spent so much time in private, quiet worship at St Mary's, it seemed only right that he should preserve her place there, and he joined her now on Sundays, their spirits together in comfort.

Rita had always asked after his wife, screwing her eyes upon his face. He thought her cold-blooded, the way she slunk about the room, stripping slowly, slithering to and fro before the bed where he waited. The white skin rippling, the surprising contours of her breasts on that lean, lithe body. He asked her to be still but she had to do her dance every time. The murderous Mars of her mouth, the darting eyes, black as diesel. When he had her pinned, she writhed and whipped in all directions. That's why he tied her down. When she protested, he stopped up her mouth. He made her submit to him. He made them all submit, every single girl.

'I could have been a nurse,' Rita told him, but the money was no good, she said. She kept a nurse's uniform in her cupboard. She wore it once when he asked. She took his temperature with an oversized glass thermometer. 'You're hot. Too hot to handle.' She always made him feel as if she were laughing at him. He let her know who was in charge.

In later years, after a long career in brothels, Gillies had gone soft about the women who worked for him. He wanted them looked after when he was gone. They would stay in the houses, he decided. Mr Wye had dismissed the notion. 'You can't do that,' he said. 'It's an absurd idea. Don't be ridiculous. Keep them in the houses? Doing what? Just living there? It doesn't suit a man to be sentimental.'

Gillies turned square on him, his face contorted. 'Sentimental?'

Mr Wye continued unperturbed. 'It is my duty, as your legal adviser, to ensure you make sound business decisions. If you were to let out the houses, there would be tax benefit, plus the rental income—'

Gillies did not let him finish. 'They've earned me a fortune. Who else will look after them? They've not got families, most of them, or the wrong kind of family, if they do. It's no skin off my nose, letting them see out their golden years under a solid roof.'

'And then what?'

'What?'

'What happens then? We can't get them out, once they're in. They'll have dependents – some of them have children already, hidden away, or they'll get a lodger in – a

39

sitting tenant, that's right, impossible to shift, or you'll have a hefty legal bill if you do. You haven't thought this through.' Mr Wye put his handkerchief to his forehead.

Neither of them spoke for a few minutes. They regarded each other, one squat and heavyset, glowering, all eyebrows, and the solicitor, so tall and narrow, dressed like a Puritan in black and white.

'As you wish,' Mr Wye finally said, and by the end of the week, Gillies' stable of madams and whores had become legal tenants in some of the best neighbourhoods in London. It galled him to do it. For a long time after, he made those girls pay. He went through them as if ticking off a list: methodically, brutally. He took them from behind so as not to see their fear.

Twenty-five years later he stood on the doorstep of the house in the Crescent, feeling their eyes on him. What an old bag Rita was. If he offered her the right amount, showed her his wallet, he bet that she would do it right there on the spot. Once a whore, always a whore, that's what he said.

Rita would submit to him, and so would the other one, and the boy as well, Joseph Gribble, son of Sal. The shut door before him would open – every last door, every whore.

On the train home to Kettering, Mr Wye reviewed his notes. There were twenty houses in all, which made for a considerable estate, even derelict – at least a million each, likely more in the current market. No wonder Marie Gillies was keen to sell up the lot.

4

Until then, Marie Gillies had lived an ordinary life. There was the small terraced house decorated in magnolia throughout; the clothes that were the same as other people wore, their colours muted, autumnal even in spring and summer; the meat and two veg for her tea. Life was as she expected it to be. People never remembered her name. Her colleagues regularly forgot her birthday – it seemed that every year there was a last-minute scuffle behind the register, a card produced at the end of the day, signed in a hurry even though she had worked at the Linen Cupboard for more than thirty years. She went to the same cinema every week and the usher – always a spotty man called Greg whose cheeks wept when he shaved – looked at her blankly. The greengrocer barely took her in over a fistful of change; the butcher forgot she liked her bacon smoked, with plenty of fat; the baker never held back the lemon-almond loaf she asked for, only baked on Thursday and always sold out before lunch.

What was it? She was so ordinary as to be invisible: a

short, overweight, middle-aged woman with peering, cre-
puscular eyes under heavy brows that were stitched
together. Her father's eyes. An obstinate set to her mouth
– she had a gummy smile, having softened her molars with
sugar. She was not pretty and never had been; a lifetime of
thinking she was not pretty had made her decidedly so. She
had a habit of sneaking: she stashed sweets and chocolates
and crisps in her room, not necessarily things she wasn't
allowed but things she didn't feel she *should* have and, feeling that, she took them all the more. It came naturally to her
to conceal, sweating in her efforts not to be found out. She
looked furtive now, sitting in a chair in the bank lobby.
People did not like to look at her.

It was Saturday morning and the bank was busy. Marie
had already waited a good twenty minutes, watching other
customers come and go. She figured the cashier had forgotten her. Five more minutes and she would be off – she would
leave it, try another day, or perhaps she would not bother at
all. She waited five minutes, and another five for good measure. Only as she was gathering her shopping – the buns
roofed with pink sugar that her mother loved, a reel of white
cotton for mending vests, some wine gums and three gossip
magazines full of slimming tips and the latest health warn-
ings – did a young man appear before her. She had seen him
a moment before shoving a Mars bar into his mouth. When
he smiled, chocolate spittle loop-de-looped his teeth. 'Miss
Gillies?' He was perhaps twenty-five years old, very slight,
with thin hair that curtained his ears. His suit was too big.
He wore a shiny tie the colour of plastic babydoll skin and

patent-leather shoes, ostentatiously pointed – she didn't understand the fashion. He was friendly enough, though, guiding Marie down a corridor and into a cubicle with just enough room for a desk and two chairs.

'Tea or coffee?' Marie shook her head. 'Glass of water?'

'I just want to ask about getting some money. For a holiday.'

'A holiday. How nice. Where is it you're thinking of going?'

'Italy. With my mother. It's a surprise for her. That's why I've come on my own.' Marie pulled some documents from her handbag. 'I've saved a bit, but there's another account I've never used.' She hesitated; she wasn't sure how right it was, what she was doing.

The young man had seated himself, with great flourish, at a computer screen. 'May I?' he said, indicating her papers. He tapped with two fingers. The placard on his desk said Douglas Smart. She studied his name, resolved to memorize it, just in case. She had her father's artful instincts in her, whether she knew it or not.

Douglas Smart licked his teeth. He couldn't have been more different from the elderly bank manager, Mr Dagger-Davis, who had visited Marie and her mother at home after her father's death. That man had been grey, dour, quiet but firm: there was to be no change, he told them, to the way they lived. Everything had been arranged; no detail of their future had been overlooked. There would be a monthly allowance for all the necessities, as there had always been. Every bill – the gas and water, electric, phone, council tax, house insurance, TV licence – would be paid by the bank. If the house needed painting, they should get in touch with the bank. If the roof needed mending, or a ceiling came crashing down, or the pipes froze, call the bank.

Marie and Flavia had looked at each other. It was to be expected, really, that her father would have gone to such lengths for their care, for he had always been clear about the way he wanted things done. He was very particular. 'Just so,' Flavia said when readying the house for his return at the end of a busy week in London. If she didn't get it right, the weekend would be spoiled. It was a relief when he left for the station on Sunday afternoon and Flavia collapsed into a chair. Sometimes she went off and had a little cry in the kitchen – her red nose gave her away. Then, when she had recovered, and they had eaten their sandwiches, as they did every Sunday evening, and washed their hair, they sat side by side in front of the telly while it dried, Marie with her box of chocolates, Flavia with her sighs.

Flavia and Marie had always done as Arthur Gillies instructed, both when he was alive and dead. They posted their maintenance requests to the bank, then watched, amazed, as the money appeared in Flavia's account. They never abused this trust nor changed the way they lived. They did not need much.

But now Marie thought they needed a holiday. She wished to take her mother back to Italy, the country of her birth, just once before she died. Flavia was seventy-eight years old. It was time.

'This is not what I expected,' Douglas Smart said, interrupting her thoughts. He looked at his computer screen with a certain wonder, shaking his head, then turned to Marie, looking her up and down as if to compute what he saw.

She stammered something about a mistake. The trip was an extravagance; she knew that, but she thought they could afford it, if they were careful. They would try to stay with family, and she heard the convents were cheap. 'I know Mr Dagger-Davis said we must only use the account for the house,' Marie said. She promised she would save more of what she earned, for she frittered away her wage packet every week.

'I need to speak to someone about this,' Douglas Smart said.

Marie gripped her handbag. 'I only wanted to—'

'Your trip to Italy won't be a problem. You can have any kind of holiday you want, by the looks of things. Why not buy a villa while you're there?' He turned his computer screen towards her.

'I don't understand,' Marie said.

Douglas Smart wrinkled his brow. 'You mean to say you didn't know about these funds?'

'What funds? What are funds?'

'Funds are money. This is your money.'

'Money?' Marie needed her specs, which hung around her neck. When she looked at the computer screen, she couldn't believe it. So many numbers – there were millions. She and Flavia had millions in the bank.

The next hour passed in a blur. She didn't recall much of

what Douglas Smart said because the top of her head seemed to have come off. There was a jet engine in the cubicle with them, circling, wishing to land, drowning all sound with its engine. She tried to compose herself. She smiled, nodding as if she understood the intricacies of the accounts. When she left, she forgot her handbag and shopping and he had to come after her. Marie's eyes, when she thanked him, shone with tears.

Her feet knew the way home. She arrived at her own door and somehow the key went in, despite her shaking hands. She stood on Flavia's flowered carpet, chanting, 'Toast, toast.' It was the only thing she could say. Flavia helped her get her coat off. Marie stepped out of her shoes – Flavia took those as well, and there were Marie's sheepskin slippers on the radiator. She went and sat down at the kitchen table. She was aware of her mother moving in the background, bending and straightening, looking in the oven, resetting saucepans, gliding round the kitchen, her movements smoothed by repetition. She heard Flavia's knife on the board, smelled toast, then four slices appeared, thick with butter and jam, and a cup of hot, sweet tea slid the length of the table.

Marie didn't speak, just ate and drank. Flavia laid a hand on her shoulder. 'Lunch soon,' she said. Behind her, on the sideboard, stood the cut-glass decanter, still half full of the whisky that had been her father's tipple, and a bottle of the claret he favoured. Flavia kept both wiped clean of dust, on display, ready to pour. Marie stared at the bottles.

She thought that perhaps, for the first time in her life, she could do with a drink.

Just like the loaves and fishes, the money was. Water into wine – a miracle.

*

Flavia cooked always, all week, every meal fresh and hot: fry-ups, soups and casseroles served with fresh loaves; delicious suppers, the meat tender, stewed for hours, or beaten thin and pan-fried at high heat, the breading crispy, light, clean on the tongue, neatly washed down with a cup of tea. Her sauces were intricate, thoughtful, varied – the same but different. The red sauce. The white sauce. Sauces for fish, for white fish, oily fish, pink fish, and for meat: the reduction, the glaze, the gravy gathered. Dripping collected in a pan. Trotters and tongue. Crackling – all kinds of skin. A chicken in half, snapping the wishbone when she split the ribcage, and the parson's nose: she saved it for herself, for the end of the meal, and ate it whole in one fatty mouthful. Marie liked to gnaw the greasy wings; they divided the heart, poached in vegetable broth.

On Saturday and Sunday, Flavia's meal preparations filled the whole of the morning. She got into the habit when Arthur was alive and only home at weekends and holidays. She made him something nice. After he died, she kept the habit. She was up early, laying out what she'd bought on Friday, dealing with the bones herself, chopping, seasoning, flouring; a plate for this, a bowl for that, the old oven warming up, the element ticking. They ate generous roasts of pork and duck and chicken, leg of lamb that was too much for two but somehow they got through it, or a deep, rich game pie, beef Wellington, Lancashire hotpot. Always pudding – a cake, carefully frosted, or trifle, apple tart with custard, tiramisu. Marie usually had a lie-in on Saturday and ate her breakfast while Flavia cleaned the heavy pan in which she'd already fried onions and garlic, the skillet still hot as she scoured it with salt and threw in a handful of water that spattered. Then she oiled the pan again to get on with the meal. Marie licked the cake spoon, or had a go at whipping cream, but always Flavia finished the job, her arm a blur.

Ever since she could remember, it had always been the same: Flavia and Marie, Marie and Flavia. As a little girl, when Flavia was in the room, Marie had eyes for no one else. She trailed her mother around the house. They were all mixed up together, she and Flavia, devoted – yes, that's what they were, *devoted*, with no friends to speak of, the neighbours still keeping their distance after fifty-five years in the same road. Flavia and Marie felt alike about things; they rarely disagreed. They didn't even bicker. They understood each other. They were hardly separate, rarely apart.

Marie laid the table with a cloth and napkins, knives, forks, spoons, mugs for their tea. Flavia hung up her apron and patted her hair. There they sat, facing each other. Arthur's place had always been at the head of the table, the chair with the red cushion, which they still regarded as his chair and avoided sitting in. Flavia poured the tea and said a quick, silent prayer of thanks – Marie saw her lips moving. They ate without speaking, their only noises in appreciation of what went in, chewing with their mouths open to keep the air flowing. They refilled their plates as often as they pleased. They ate until it was all gone, until they could hardly move.

Then, slowly but surely, Flavia started on the washing-up and Marie dried, both of them belching quietly into their sleeves and apologizing. The worktops were wiped, the floor swept and Marie went off to watch telly.

'You OK?' Flavia said, following her into the sitting room.

'What?'

'You sick?'

'Why do you say that, Ma?'

'You're quiet. You sick?'

Marie shook her head.

'You look pale. You better rest. Work makes you tired,' Flavia said. 'You want me run it?'

'What?'

'The bath. You want me run it?'

'I'm fine, Ma.'

Always fine, her girl. *Ave Maria* – that was her lips moving again. Flavia was reassured.

*

Marie went into the bathroom and closed the door. It was a relief to be alone. She stood before the mirror. For once she wanted to see herself. Did she look different? Not in her face, but in her eyes: a glint. A match lit down a mineshaft, beginning to climb.

Flavia was outside the bathroom door. Her shuffle, in slippers, to get nearer. 'I don't hear water. You OK? You tired?'

'No. Yes. Yes, I'm tired.'

'I going to watch telly. You come down after your bath.'

'OK.'

'What?'

'I said yes.' What else could she say?

'OK.'

She heard her mother's hobbling tread on the stairs – her limp, the bad hip, pain she bore silently but with that look of suffering. Then the mug clunking down, a fuss of cushions rearranged. Soon the voices of soap characters, people they didn't know but who were so familiar, rang out loud and clear. Almost as if they were there.

Marie left the bath running and went to her room. She paced, thinking about the money. Money that would fill the airless house from floor to ceiling, stacked notes in bank vaults, mountains of money, millions of pounds. Who could she tell? Who would believe her? Even Flavia would say she was mad. It would be her secret, she decided. It had been her father's secret and now it would be hers. Oh, to be rich, she had often thought, and said it, too. Who didn't? When she was young, what she would do if she were rich had been a fantasy that filled the hours, always a vision of toys and sweets and a mansion with tellies in every room. As she grew older, the list included a car – the latest convertible – and holidays abroad like she saw in magazines, nice clothes, furs and jewels, the usual things that millionaires bought. Diamond earrings like headlamps. She looked at the rich people who came into the Linen Cupboard and envied them their ease. They didn't even check to see what things cost, just bought what they wanted and then some. They could afford to be tempted. New pool towels. Egyptian cotton bed sheets. Irish linen stiff as a nun's habit, the edges whipped with tiny, even stitches.

She was rich. It was better than beautiful, and Marie would never be beautiful. But being rich made her *something*. She was worth something. People would look at her and know; they would respect her, value her. They would want her money. Money made the world turn, everyone said so.

Marie took the length of the room in five strides, the width in three. She crossed to the window and looked out: the sun shone brilliantly.

It was not that they had ever wanted for anything. They were not materialistic. Flavia's jewellery was simple – her wedding band, a gold crucifix on a chain, a wristwatch Arthur had given her, the pearl earrings that had been her grandmother's, yellowed and pitted with age. Marie had expressed no great desire for things while her father was alive – she didn't dare – and he was not the type to spoil his daughter. For himself, he bought what he needed and nothing more: flannel trousers, polo shirts and jackets the same as every other man, in grey and navy blue, nothing remarkable, although he wore a nice suit for work. He would arrive in his suit every Friday and promptly hand it over to Flavia's care for the weekend. She would sponge the suit, wash and starch and press his shirt, wipe his shoes and polish them. Then on Sunday, after lunch, when he had slept it off, he would change into his suit and, without delay, say goodbye. There was nothing unusual in him going, so used to it were they; all of Marie's life he had worked in London. He would walk to the end of their road and catch a bus to the station just as any other person would do – but a rich man wouldn't. A rich man would have a driver, at the very least a car. They had no car. A rich man would travel the world. Her father never wanted to go anywhere; he only wished to stay at home and eat, nap, stroll the garden. No, there was nothing Marie could think of to show that he'd had money in the bank. The usual things she associated with wealth – giant wristwatches, a big house, a Rolls-Royce – were simply not there.

But they were rich. They were rich! She whispered it to herself. Her hands were clapping of their own accord. She lurched drunkenly, missing a step. Marie caught hold of the chest of drawers when she landed and it banged against the wall. Felt good. She rocked the chest hard, drawers sucking in and out like waves on a shore. One drawer slid out and crashed down, spilling socks across the floor, and that is when Flavia burst in.

'The bath,' she cried.

Marie groaned.

'What the noise about? You hurt? What? You hurt yourself?'

Marie nodded. She pointed down.

'Too much lunch,' said her mother. 'I told you, hot bath. Hot bath feels good. You get in the bath now.'

*

Tucked up in bed with a hot-water bottle, Marie rested. Flavia said she must be poorly. There was a mug of Horlicks on the bedside table, a pile of toast. Sleep, Flavia told her, rubbing her back. But Marie couldn't sleep. She was remembering.

He was a booming voice at the weekend. He was a reason to stay quiet indoors, to mind her table manners, tiptoe on the stairs. Never make a mess or fuss, never laugh, try not to cry. She had been frightened of him when she was little but still she held his hand and pecked his cheek when he wanted her to – his kisses rubbed like sandpaper. He told her to pull up her socks, tuck in her blouse, close her mouth; there was nothing to be gained in going about slack-jawed, he said. She listened. She did as she was told. She kept her distance.

Who was her father? He was Arthur Gillies – that was his name. But who had he been? She never much cared, except that he was her father and she loved him. She had to. She feared him more.

But then, they hardly saw him, working in London as he did. He was a businessman preoccupied with business.

Once, when Marie asked him what kind of business, he said she wouldn't understand. That kind of talk was for men, he said. She accepted his explanation and never bothered him about it again. Marie couldn't recall ever hearing her mother ask her father a question, apart from the usual: how was his dinner? Was the meat cooked the way he liked it? Did he fancy a bit of cake? Nice bit of cake for him? Flavia hovered with the whisky decanter, the claret. Back and forth, back and forth and back again. Would that be all? Another drop? A cup of tea perhaps? She scurried around on mouse feet and Marie picked up the habit. They bustled, they hid. They gave him what he wanted: peace and quiet.

At sixteen, Marie left school to work. Her father told her she must work, must earn her keep, and listed a range of jobs he thought would suit her – the usual sort of thing for a young woman: secretary, receptionist, cashier. *Not* waitress, nor was she to go anywhere near a stage – not that she was likely to, being a large girl with a flattened face and pores that drank Max Factor. The stage had never occurred to her. She didn't know why he said it, except that there was a neighbourhood girl who had set off one day for London and never been seen again. People said she was a dancer – they gave that knowing look when they said it.

Work, he said. Work hard. Keep *quiet*.

She worked. She took a job at the Linen Cupboard. All day long she folded bed sheets and eiderdowns and cot blankets. She plumped pillows. She straightened a rainbow array of flannels. With clean hands, she laid out fine, thin hand towels for inspection, beautifully embroidered with twining vines and coronets, just for guests. Speciality items such as that didn't sell except for trousseau lists.

Marie never had a trousseau list.

If her parents had hoped she would marry, they never said. No one fancied her. She didn't like to dance, she had hair everywhere, a foreign mother and her father growled like a bear. She had never been kissed. She had crushes, entirely inappropriate: the postman who delivered to the Linen Cupboard, the greengrocer's son, the handsome young vicar who caused a sensation in town just by opening his mouth – it didn't matter what came out. Over the years the dream of love slipped away and she worked through it all, never missed a day. Her hands flew, patting, tucking, smoothing, sorting, ringing the till, giving change, every day the same. The years lined up like gravestones. Five years, then ten, twenty. She carried on working just to show her father she was made of the right stuff. Thirty years, five days a week, at the Linen Cupboard.

Flavia was at the bedroom door, looking in on her. Marie pretended to be asleep. She wanted to be alone. She needed to think. Flavia toddled off, snuffed out the hall light. Nighttime settled like a dead man's hands. Marie didn't sleep a wink.

*

On Monday, during her lunch break, she returned to the bank. She asked for Douglas Smart, who looked panicked when he saw her. Might they just go into his office for a word, she said – Marie had rehearsed the speech countless times in her head. Douglas Smart told her that in future she should speak only to Mr Dagger-Davis; he would see if Mr Dagger-Davis were free. He excused himself and she watched as he bolted down the corridor, silly shoes flapping and slipping.

Mr Dagger-Davis appeared: the stale old gentleman who had come to the house when her father died. He escorted her into *his* office, larger and grander than Douglas Smart's cubicle, decently furnished. There she was informed that his young colleague had made a mistake. He, Mr Dagger-Davis, had been out of the bank on Saturday, most unfortunate.

'Things are not as they seem,' he said.

'What do you mean?'

'The account details you saw are confidential.'

'It's my father's money.'

'That's right. Your father's accounts are held in trust. The figures you saw are your father's accounts.'

'But I'm his daughter. His only child. That's my money – my mother's money. It's ours.'

Mr Dagger-Davis looked at her with a certain patience. 'Your income is based on the interest of the trust only. You don't have access to the capital. It's not yours. You are a beneficiary of the trust. That is the arrangement.'

'The arrangement beneficiary?' Marie did not understand – not yet.

'Your father made provision for you and your mother through a trust.'

'He didn't tell us we were millionaires!'

Mr Dagger-Davis blanched. 'The accounts are private. You were not meant to see them – my colleague's mistake, as I said. If you need to speak with someone in more detail about the *legality* of this matter, I suggest you get in touch with Mr Wye, your father's solicitor.' The old man stood and reached for her hand. 'A pleasure to see you again.'

Once more Marie stumbled out of the bank. Her lunch break was nearly over, so she hurried back to the Linen Cupboard, where she spent the rest of the afternoon steaming tea towels. *Gathering* herself.

She remembered Mr Wye. Like Mr Dagger-Davis, he had been there when her father died. Both men had presented themselves as old friends of her father, although neither Flavia nor Marie had met them before. They came to the house, extended their condolences and eventually sat down, each with a cup of tea and a slice of Flavia's cherry loaf before him. There were things for Flavia to sign, the usual sort of paperwork, Mr Wye had explained. Once the estate was in order – that was the phrase used by both Mr Dagger-Davis and Mr Wye – the gentlemen disappeared again and life as Flavia and Marie knew it resumed, unchanged except that Arthur Gillies no longer returned at the weekends or for holidays.

Fifteen years had passed since her father's death. It seemed no time at all, looking back on it. Marie wondered how it went so unnoticeably. She was not one to pause on the stairs at the end of the day and think, *There it goes, out with the lights.* But fifteen years – that was a lot of life.

She made an appointment to see Mr Wye. She got the

time off work – an unusual request for her, but Marie insisted. She did not tell anyone where she was going, not even her mother. She arrived early and was seen right away, perched on a slender chair that was much too small for her.

'Your father,' said Mr Wye, and then paused. He looked eighty, at least, and she wondered why he had not yet retired. When he spoke, though, his voice was strong. 'Your father and I worked together for a long time. It was a sad day for us all when he died.' He cleared his throat and looked right at her. 'What can I do for you, Miss Gillies?'

'I was at the bank,' she began, and then stopped, shocked with sudden emotion. *Choked up.* Mr Wye waited. Marie tried to speak but found she could not.

'You should have all you need, you and your mother. If you want to go on holiday that's fine with us,' Mr Wye said, not gently. 'There are funds for that. Write to the bank in the usual way. Mr Dagger-Davis has been in touch and he said you are certain of going. Miss Gillies, you may plan your trip.'

'I know there's money, millions of money,' Marie blurted. 'I saw it with my own eyes.'

Mr Wye sighed.

'Why didn't we know about the money?'

'Your father set up a trust to look after you. His instructions were that you should continue to live in the way to which you were accustomed.'

'My mother doesn't know.'

'Your father—'

'I want my money!'

'Your father did not expect you to ask questions about the way he did things.'

Marie paused to consider this. 'Where did he get the money?'

'He earned it. He was a good businessman.'

'I don't even know what kind of business he was in,' she admitted. 'He didn't really talk when he was home. He was always tired. He just wanted to rest.' It had never troubled her before that she didn't know what her father did to earn a living. There seemed a general sort of work to be done by men, mostly in offices, sometimes in meetings, not very interesting, and that's what she thought her father did. Business was business – that's what he said. Not for her head.

Mr Wye hesitated. 'He owned property. In London. He bought property cheaply after the war. He was clever. He was ahead of everyone.'

'How much property?'

'A good number of houses. He rebuilt what had been bombed, he modernized – he was always modernizing, bringing things up to date. He was very proud of what he'd achieved.'

'Houses?'

'Rather a lot of them.' Mr Wye looked at his hands, slowly opened and closed the fingers. The joints clicked. If he pinched the skin, it would hold in a peak once released.

'He still owns them?'

'Yes.'

'Even when he's dead?'

Mr Wye snorted. 'They are held in trust. It's not unusual.'

'Then we own them,' Marie concluded.

'Not quite. Not yet.'

'When?'

Mr Wye cleared his throat. 'It's not for me to say.'

'Why won't you tell me anything?'

'Miss Gillies, I cannot—'

'I just don't understand.'

'You don't *need* to understand, if I may be so blunt—'

'I want you to tell me.'

'Tell you what?'

'Whose houses are they?'

'Miss Gillies—'

'Who lives in the houses?'

'It's not for me—'

'Who lives there?'

Old friends of her father, he finally told her. They were mostly very old – some were probably dead, he thought. 'I must check on them soon. I do from time to time.'

'My father pays to keep his friends in houses in London?' She could hardly believe what she was saying.

'Yes.'

The ample flesh across Marie's shoulders and back prickled in goose pimples; the signal connected with her thighs, which clenched. Her toes curled and both hands cramped with gripping so hard. 'Why?' she managed to ask.

'That,' said Mr Wye, 'is a long story.'

5

Joseph missed the solicitor, Mr Wye, because he was out, making his rounds. Joseph didn't work, although making his rounds could take four or five hours of his day, depending on the buses. For more than thirty years he had diligently ridden the London buses, every single one. The routes and timetables were in his head; he rode them all, though he had his favourites.

He began at the newsagent, where he bought the *Daily Mail*, then progressed, at a slug's pace, to Camden via the canal, taking in the ever-changing scenery of the water: oily one day, foaming and spidery the next, or speckled with blossoms. The water undulated rubbish. He didn't know how deep it was. He half expected a body, but all these years had passed and the worst he'd seen was a wingless, bleating seagull, not yet dead.

Leaving the canal, Joseph caught a bus. Often he started with the 29 to Trafalgar Square and went from there, it being an axis of sorts. Once aboard the bus of his choice, he enjoyed its gentle swaying and shudders. He listened to the bus grunting up the hills, same as his body called out as he exerted himself, and he leaned and clenched on the corners. When the bus sat, he, too, was at ease; then both inhaled and rumbled on again. The bus was a balm to him. What he saw and heard he kept to himself: proof of other small lives being lived all around. People swallowed tablets at prescribed hours, had quiet chats with themselves or gazed at family photos, remembering who they were. Watching them, he felt he was part of life. He nodded as the seat next to him emptied and filled. He replied when necessary, but never more than a halting word or two, having his stutter to contend with. He disembarked for lunch, then climbed back on to return home for mid to late afternoon, depending on the traffic and how far he'd travelled.

That's what he did. He'd been riding the buses daily since he was a teenager, but they had always interested him, from when he was a boy. He couldn't say why. Mama took him on the bus when he was small and it felt like an occasion. They would go somewhere – it didn't matter where – and he would mark it on the correct timetable. He had all the timetables; Mama and the other ladies collected them for him. Mama would often doze on the bus, holding his hand while he looked out of the window, and he would shake her awake when it was their stop, satisfied with having pulled the bell himself.

As he grew older, the bus was his escape. After school, at the weekends, off he went. Mama seemed relieved to have him occupied. It kept him out of the house. She didn't like him there when she had customers. It wasn't good for business to have a child around, even though he was grown up by then; when he was little he had been more easily hidden. Men came to Mama to get away from their affairs, including children, so many of them not being fond of prattle. All those men hanging around the stairs when he went up to hide in his room after a day out on the buses, arms over his head to muffle his ears – Joseph knew why they were there. He turned on the radio, not too loud so as not to disturb the atmosphere. He stayed in his room all night, hating even to use the toilet; he never flushed lest he made a sound and someone heard and would want to investigate and think they'd seen a ghost.

Soon Joseph was skipping school to ride the buses and no one noticed. Mama saw that he was happier and that was enough. Making his rounds, she called it. He watched the city change before his eyes. Buildings went up and down and up again; spare acres were erased to make more homes, more shops. He saw crimes committed: a man laid flat with a plank, battery, muggings in broad daylight that he never mentioned to a soul. He saw Prince Philip's profile in a speeding car more than once, all traffic stopped by the police to let him through the junctions. He saw the Queen wave as she left the Royal Hospital Chelsea. He saw the endless flowers when the princess died.

It's not that he had money and therefore his time was his to spend as he pleased, but he did have a house in which to live rent-free, a house for which he had not paid, and he had a bank account that was replenished regularly, seemingly from beyond. He had never lived anywhere else, at least that he could remember, and the house became his when Mama died, simple as that. Annetta called it his house, and so did Rita. No mention of anyone else. In the six years since his mother's death, nothing had occurred to make him think otherwise. Six years of peace, of sorts, and now in his pocket he had a letter he dared not let out of sight. *Duce Glib & Blythe Solicitors wish to inquire of the tenants living in 12, The Crescent, on behalf of the estate of Arthur Gillies,* signed by Thomas Wye.

Joseph knew what the man wanted – instinctively he knew. But the house was part of the agreement between Mama and Arthur Gillies, so she had sworn on her death-bed, just as Joseph was part of the agreement between his mother and what she did for a living. Unlike the others who got pregnant, she would bear her son, and at his birth she made the promise of mothers: to keep him safe from harm.

The 253 accelerated along an open stretch, hoovering leaves and nearly a cyclist, who shook his fist. The bus ate flies and feathers and drank rainwater. It belched, farted exhaust, came to a halt. Passengers got off. More got on. There was a struggle with the pushchairs: who was there first, who would have to wait for the next bus. A pushchair got off in a huff. The bus nosed into traffic – they were on their way. All day Joseph rode and tried to relax. He felt for Mr Wye's letter, just to be sure, and checked his pocket again before he disembarked in Camden.

They couldn't take it away from him. They just couldn't. Especially when he had so little – all Joseph had in the world was the house and the people in it.

He walked to the Crescent without looking around himself. He found Rita waiting at the door, ready to be off. She told him that Annetta was asleep upstairs, best left undisturbed, locked in as usual. There – Rita pointed to a wall peppered with nails – hung the key. Tea was in the oven.

He'd better keep an eye out, she warned Joseph. He nodded and went downstairs to the kitchen, where he helped himself to biscuits.

At five o'clock he ate his tea. Annetta still hadn't peeped so Joseph cleaned her plate as well and piled the dishes in the sink for Rita to wash tomorrow.

He watched telly.

He stood outside Annetta's door before he retired: nothing. She was in there. She couldn't have escaped. The key hung undisturbed on its nail downstairs. She was going nowhere.

'G-g-g-good n-n-n-n-night,' he whispered.

*

It was not the alarm that set her off – although it did make Rita jump through her skin every morning, as if she didn't know it was coming – but the effort of getting her blouse off the hanger. The flimsy plastic hanger, one of many in cheerful, insipid colours: Marigold, Blue Heaven, Pink Cadillac, Rhododendron, Green Lagoon and Holly Berry Glow. She had thrown herself from bed at the bleep and twitched the duvet into place before her eyes were even open. She bathed, chewed her toast, drank her tea, feeling steady, not too bad at all, considering the evening. A bottle of sweet sherry opened at five on the dot, supper of boiled cod and oven chips on a tray in front of the telly, the bottle drunk by ten, then bed. Her usual evening at home.

The wardrobe doors drooped from their hinges like bad teeth. Rita wanted a blouse and there were plenty, a whole lifetime of blouses, a good fifty years' worth. She chose the pink georgette that wouldn't crease and flicked at the top button. It popped off like a bottle cap and the blouse collapsed backwards at the shock. She chose another blouse, not so pressed, with a tie all in knots. The next, a pale floral print, showed a mustard-coloured stain on the left breast; a fourth, woollen, in cream, was the wrong season.

A deadly feeling clamped down on Rita like a lid; a fire lit. Something scrabbled to get out, something red-hot with claws and a skin of spikes. Oh, she got cross, she did. Rita needed to pick a fight. The blouses still on hangers shuddered when she kicked at the wardrobe; some slid like broken eggs to the floor. Her tantrum blowing full, she began to kill the blouses one by one, cracking hangers as easily as babies' forearms. We will die in here, she thought. They would die, she and the blouses, and the long-legged spiders that seemed to double in size every time they swallowed a fly, and the money plant in the corner, over-watered and rotting inside. 'Die,' she said. 'Die, die, die.'

She was dressing for lunch with Edward. He was the kind of man she had been used to a long time ago: upper class, arrogant. She needed, in the next ten minutes, to dress for him in a way that complemented his quiet, classic, inoffensive style. She pictured him in well-cut navy gabardine, leaning in to whisper to her as they shopped together at Peter Jones after lunch – a token for her, a gesture of what was to come. A silk scarf, or a pair of leather gloves. Sensible, beautiful, just intimate enough. His mahogany-coloured hair crested in waves across his head: cultivated hair, brushed until it shone, pruned without looking just-cut.

If only Edward would marry her.

If he would just *marry* her. She was ready to marry again. She wasn't choosy. They were, these men she met, every one of them, good enough to strike a bargain with. Keep it light, keep it moving, that's what she told herself when sizing up any potential husband over a table for two in Covent Garden or Soho.

If one of those men would marry her and give her a house—

William walked out of her life three weeks ago. *William* and his wonderful house in Belgravia, where he would be dashing around right now, a cup of tea steaming on the bureau in his dressing room, a pressed shirt slipping neatly from its wooden hanger. Now he was choosing his tie. Now he was leaving the house for an appointment at his club or with his tailor or shoemaker. A car waited outside. The housekeeper reclaimed the cup and saucer from the bureau and upended both in the dishwasher. The dishwasher – how she longed for a dishwasher, and a housekeeper, and a waiting car. *William* was seventy-six years old, a confirmed bachelor, but Rita had married all kinds. Nothing surprised her, not least a bachelor settling down in his dotage. They thought they wanted a woman half their age, but what did those women know? She heard they shaved their private parts and behaved like pornographic film stars in the bedroom. There was no art, no elegance in such behaviour.

Rita had retained her elegance, of that she could be sure.

Of course she had met *William* and Edward and Charles and Giles and Sebastian – and George, Harry, Andrew, Mick, Vincent, Anthony, Peter, and the Spaniard, Marco – through her personal ad. That was how to meet a man these days. *Attractive, well-spoken older woman seeks someone to dine with.* She had done it for years and it was a nice little earner. Dinner, then a room somewhere.

The phone rang and she jumped – how she jumped! Right out of her skin. Rita was all nerves today. She must have slept badly, although she didn't recall waking in the night. She answered, listened, sighed. 'I'll be there quick as I can.'

*

Joseph didn't know how she did it, but she did. Like Houdini. He went to bed safe in the knowledge that she was locked up for the night and he woke in the morning to find she was gone. Her door was open and there was no Annetta in bed, no Annetta downstairs wanting breakfast. The kettle was cold. The front door creaked in the breeze – she'd left it ajar for anyone to walk right in and take what they wanted, and all that time Joseph was asleep upstairs, oblivious.

He phoned Rita right away. The key to Annetta's room still hung on its nail. He would show it to Rita when she arrived, proof that he had done as he was told. He knew she wouldn't believe him. He didn't believe it himself: how a person opened a door that was locked from the outside – unless it hadn't been locked in the first place. Joseph would never dare suggest *that* to Rita, when it was Rita who had locked Annetta's bedroom door.

He looked again, to be sure – he looked in every room, even the cupboard that housed the water pipes. No Annetta.

He'd had a goldfish once. He didn't know why he thought of it then but he did. When he was eight, one of Rita's boy-friends brought him a goldfish he called Noisy – he liked the joke, even if no one else got it. Noisy had crimson lips and a silver-sequinned body and circled his bowl in endless figure of eights. Joseph took great care of him, watching him swim for hours on end. Noisy died one day while he was at school. He hid Noisy's bowl in the cupboard that housed the water pipes and cried about it when he was alone, but he never told anyone, not even Mama. After a week, the water was thick with scum and bits of black lint hung in streamers from Noisy floating on top. There was a very bad smell coming off – Mama would soon sniff it out on one of her inspections of the house. He waited until everyone was occupied that night, then carried Noisy's bowl outside and left it on the front pavement. In the morning, Noisy was gone and no one could figure out how the fishbowl got there. Impossible. Mama always had one eye on the front door and swore she wouldn't have missed it. Rita thought it was a punter playing a trick. Annetta thought it was a ghost. Joseph never told them. He let them believe what they wanted.

*

Well, Rita was fond of saying. Well. Never mind. If no one's going to do it. Well, she said again, and paused. She waited. Well. She knew what would happen: she would do it herself.

'Well?'

Joseph looked at his shoes: there was bacon grease across the top of one. He had size ten feet, wide as planks, and wore regular black brogues from Marks and Spencer. His grey flannel trousers and navy-blue polo shirt came from there, too. He looked just like his father, especially now that he'd lost most of his hair. It was uncanny. Sometimes she caught sight of him and thought it was Arthur Gillies himself standing before her – her heart skipped and she felt suddenly at sea, until she realized it was only Joseph.

'Not back then, is she? The minx. How'd she get away this time?'

He shrugged.

'You need to keep an eye out. I'm only repeating myself, wasting my breath. Never mind. Not your fault, is it? Never is.' Rita passed him her handbag. She turned and faced the park. 'Well. Here I go. You put the kettle on. That's the least you can do.'

First the swings and sandpit, then a slow turn around the park's lower basin, checking all the benches. Nothing. Rita's heart sank: she must climb the hill, for Annetta was drawn to the wilder, lonely reaches where teenagers lurked with cigarettes and aerosols and dogs ran off the lead. Rita despised the dogs especially, the way they came at her as if about to leap and latch on and knock her down all in one go. Or they stopped dead in the path; stopped and raised a leg, swizzle pouring out just where her foot had meant to step. Worse yet, the big dogs simply defecated before her very eyes, glaring back at her as if nothing would stop them. Labradors and sheepdogs and Rottweilers, stuffed with meaty chunks, and the small dogs, too, lost on a fat lap but leaping into her path as she approached, teeth bared, snapping at her ankles. *Yappity yappity. Yappity yappity.* Never-ending.

The sun was high as she began her ascent – the heat took it out of her and Rita unbuttoned her coat. She took care on the tarmac, baked soft as it was, her heels sinking and sticking. She didn't want to fall; sometimes she did. She had confessed this to her GP after losing her balance one day when she was at the shops. An ambulance had come to carry her off to hospital but she refused to go. She got to her feet, brushed herself down and rubbed a bit of spit on her handbag where it had scraped the pavement. She was fine, she said. Just a dizzy spell, nothing to worry about. She bade the paramedic team goodbye with a wave and her best jolly voice and set off back the way she had come – never mind the shops. She would have a bit of toast for her tea. 'They don't hand out awards for independence,' one of them had called after her.

Well.

It happened again, a few weeks later. Black waves, was how she put it. Black waves in the aisle at Tesco and down she went, bruising her hip when she landed. No ambulance, she insisted. She wasn't a time-waster. There was nothing wrong with her. Fit as a fiddle, she was. A taxi would get her home just fine, and when the driver assisted her to the door of her block of flats, that was as far as she'd allow him. There was a lift, she pointed out. That's what lifts were for: people who couldn't climb stairs, for one reason or another. Lazy gits. She dragged herself into the lift and up she went, cursing under her breath all the way. For the love of Jesus. She was a silly old cow, she was. In the door and straight to bed. She couldn't even get herself a hot-water bottle, that's how bad it was. Her hip went purple and wouldn't be slept on so she turned to the other side – not her usual way to sleep, but that was life. Just get on with it. Her GP, examining her a week later, said she should use a walking stick. 'You won't catch me with one of them,' Rita cackled. 'And I'm keeping my high heels, too. They're good for my legs. Can't walk without them.'

No black waves now, just the bright midday sun blasting away. She felt perfectly well – she was the picture of health, and Rita always went out looking her best. *Click clack*. Heel, toe, bones solid, blood aflow. She didn't feel a day over forty.

There was shouting in the distance, a crowd of people gathering further along. Usually it was some drunks fighting among themselves or getting moved on. They never went quietly, did they? Rita strained her eyes, turned her good ear – it worked perfectly, while the other one felt stuffed with cotton wool. What was the commotion? A flash of nudity – Rita's eyebrows, all pencil lines, shot up.

*

How many times had it happened now? Rita tried to count as she filled the bathtub. A dozen times at least Joseph had called her in a panic because he could not find Annetta anywhere in the house. She got the key, Annetta did, and slunk out of the front door. Even the worst weather failed to stop her: she would come home soaked, shaking with cold, and no wonder, for she took off her clothes.

Annetta lay in the bath for a long time, warming through. Rita looked in every once in a while. 'Just checking,' she said. Annetta blew bubbles. She lapped bathwater and her chops dripped. Another five minutes and Rita was back, ready to rub her down with a towel. 'Stand *still*,' Rita said. She found a clean set of pyjamas and dressed her like a doll, roughly inserting her arms and legs, buttoning her up as if that would keep her in. 'Where are your clothes, Annetta?' Rita wondered aloud. Annetta took no notice of her. Her clothes were strewn across the park; a dog had run off home with her stockings; a jackdaw had her cardigan, with its brass buttons, for his nest.

Rita wiped the fog from the mirror but Annetta wasn't interested in looking at herself. She was like a person in a dream: not here but *there*. Did she notice the water draining from the bath in thirsty slurps? Did she mind when Rita stepped on her bare foot? Not at all. She allowed herself to be led downstairs, clutching a bit of Rita's skirt. Then it was a cup of tea and boiled egg and soldiers before Rita marched her back to bed and locked the door. Let her shout and pull at the knob; at least Rita knew where she was.

After that, Rita needed a sit-down. Joseph wanted to be off, she could tell. If he didn't ride a bus every day he wasn't himself. 'Never mind, I'll stay here and keep an eye on things,' she grumbled. It was just like a man not to see what needed doing but to do what he wanted. Well. And didn't she know it? She'd married all kinds, but they had the one thing in common: pure selfishness.

When she was sure that Joseph was gone, Rita hunted in her handbag for her mobile. She used it only for her personal ad. She pressed the button to turn it on. The screen flashed, that little bit of advertising. Marvellous. She waited. In a moment a message would be there – or not. She was hopeful every time.

Nothing. Well. Away it went. Never mind.

She had a headache. Usually she took a bit of sweet sherry for relief, but there was nothing to drink in the house, not since Arthur Gillies died. Over the years she had searched to the rafters, rummaged through cupboards and drawers, groped the high shelves, twitched her nose along the floorboards, seeking the trail of a bottle. Arthur was well enough preserved in the stuff in his grave, but not a drop remained in his penultimate resting place. Rita might have slipped out to the pub for a swift one, but there was Annetta to think about. 'Not on my watch,' she said aloud.

She checked the time. Three o'clock. Joseph would be gone for a couple of hours, if she knew him. She would try to relax herself. Shoes off, legs up and a blanket over her knees, just like any other granny. There. That was better. The rest of the afternoon she dozed in front of the telly. More dreams of the past, of old lovers – most of them dead by now, she was sure, though they were young, all of them, in her dreams. She thought it meant something, to dream so much of long ago. She feared she was coming to the end of her time, the past rushing up to meet her at the door. It would be equilibrium, when it ended. When *she* ended. No future, only the past, but the past a sort of nothingness, the nothing of it all being done, nothing left to do, or no chance to do it any more. Death was lightness, a dream; she in other people's dreams until they, too, came to the door and found it open.

It was only natural she should think of it. She had gone to a few funerals this year, old women she had known since they were young. She couldn't help but picture herself in the box. The way the undertaker always got it wrong when he set the mouth – she expected he would make her grin and bear it – and the yellow dress she would wear for her final destination. Clasped in one hand, a red rose. How many people would deem her enough of a friend that they must see her out? Sometimes there were only a handful of mourners at the services she went to, and Rita didn't have any children. Her husbands were all dead. Just herself and Joseph and Annetta left.

Well.

She woke when Annetta banged upstairs. 'I need to spend a penny,' she wailed. Rita led her to the bathroom and waited until she finished – Rita even wiped her bottom these days. 'I've got cold feet,' Annetta complained, so down went Rita to fill the hot-water bottle, then back up again. Oh, these tall houses, so tall and thin and cold! Rita preferred her modern flat, everything compact, the small rooms clustered around a boiler that she never turned off.

Then Annetta wanted a drink of water. Then she needed the toilet.

'But you've just been,' Rita said.

'I need the toilet,' Annetta insisted, fingering the enamel *H* that had fallen off the hot tap in the bath. Rita took the *H* and pocketed it for the junk drawer in the kitchen. So the game would renew, Rita finding the *H* in the washing or under the pillow when she changed the sheets on Annetta's bed. Back and forth the *H* changed hands, and had done these last two years, since Annetta's dementia began.

Now Annetta wanted a cup of tea. Sometimes she asked for sugar, sometimes not. It depended on what kind of day she was having. Annetta had good days and bad days. On good days it was almost like there was nothing wrong, but on bad days there were tantrums, repetition, nudity, running off. On bad days she had sugar in her tea. Rita said it only gave her energy to shout and try to get out, but she stirred in the sugar just the same, two teaspoons. Annetta wanted three but Rita said, 'Your teeth will drop out, darling.' Annetta, more often than not, grabbed at the cup and spilled half into her saucer. Just like a child, she was.

'Sugar?' Rita asked.

'Yes.'

'Yes *please*,' said Rita, but she may as well have been talking to herself. Well. Annetta sat and slurped. Rita stroked her head. She touched the docile shoulders, rested her hands, feeling the bones. Annetta was thinner; Rita could crush her. 'How's that?'

'Most kind,' Annetta mumbled.

Rita looked at her watch. Four fifteen. She slipped away and found her mobile, felt it spring to life at her touch. What a wonder it was. Sure enough, there was a missed call from Edward, her cancelled lunch. What about dinner? She phoned him straight back. Yes, she said in her message – for one was always leaving messages – dinner sounded fine, she knew the place he suggested. She would be wearing a red coat.

Something to look forward to, Rita thought, snapping the clasp of her handbag. Her horizon had opened up again, and didn't she believe in possibility? Didn't she believe in making her own luck? Didn't she just. She had guts, Rita did. Joseph would be home soon and she would be on her way into the setting sun.

She settled Annetta into bed. Then it was downstairs to put supper in the oven and do the washing-up. Rita heard a thump at the door. It was only Joseph, but still she opened the cupboard where a mirror was pasted, stuck there since the old days. She took a good look at herself, high heels tip-tapping as she turned for a side view and then the back, making sure of her curls: still there, white as sheep's wool. Her eyebrows, drawn on that morning, arced in surprise, her rouge two bright spots of excitement, her wrinkled chin whiskerless, carefully plucked. Not bad, she thought with a cluck.

*

Joseph went straight to the biscuit tin. 'Hello yourself,' Rita said. 'You'll spoil your appetite, eating those. Fancy a brew, my love?' He looked at her, chewing, his eyes soft and distant, crumbs speckling his lips. Rita chose a biscuit. 'Really, I shouldn't. There's meat pie for your tea in the oven.' She looked hard at him. She didn't need to say it, but she did anyway. 'Keep an eye out.' He avoided her gaze, nodded.

Another biscuit went in, glued to his tongue like Holy Communion. Would she never leave? He did not want to be observed as he ate. 'Well. I'm off,' Rita finally said. 'Annetta's in her room. She'll be wanting the toilet soon. Remember to lock up.' Joseph knew she didn't trust him. He heard the front door bang shut. It was always a relief when she left.

Alone, or almost alone, he enjoyed the stillness of the house; he relaxed into it as if it were his own home, his very own, and what he was doing there was being himself. His shoulders sank. His spine sagged. He took fewer steps. He did as he pleased. He ate biscuits – he piled them in, blissful biscuits, and drank tea straight from the teapot spout, holding down the lid. A person needed privacy to do that; to roam and think and mutter, if necessary. Room to be, and be nude in. Joseph had never lived on his own. He had never been left alone even for one night of his life. He was always the child in the house, although he was not a child now. He'd grown into a man and no one seemed to have noticed, the way they spoke to him. And he was getting bigger all the time, pot-bellied, fat as butter. Rita had to squeeze past him in the kitchen to get at the cupboards and cooker and sink; he was her roly-poly boy. She fussed at his clothes, pulling at them, showing him his bulges. She tapped his love handles, gave them a squeeze that tickled unpleasantly. She scolded him for leaving crumbs and snacking all the time. She rolled her eyes at him, meaning Annetta, but likewise she rolled her eyes at Annetta, meaning him, even though Annetta didn't understand at all what Rita meant, gone as she was.

The timer went. He got the meat pie out of the oven and left it to cool. There were peas on the hob. He went upstairs to let Annetta out. He unlocked the door to her room and called her name, then went downstairs and served it up: two full plates. She appeared while he was eating and stood by the table.

He enjoyed his supper, and Annetta's, too. Lately she didn't eat much, or not at all, and he often ate hers as well so that Rita wouldn't know. He put their plates in the sink and went upstairs. No need to creep, but he crept, in all his boiled whiteness. He stood at the front window, looking out. His gaze roved the park across the way, where a group of boys were clowning with a tennis ball, giddy with the heat. What weather they were having! Sunny, hot and dry all over England. People were roasting. The forecasters said it would go on all summer long. The boys in the park knew it, their antics delirious. He had missed all of that. It seemed he had always been watching, fingering the curtain edge. He wouldn't have known what to do with a ball should one pitch in his direction or, for that matter, roll directly to his toes and stop. He had never held a tennis ball, not even in a shop.

He climbed the stairs to Mama's room and sat on her bed. She had died in there: that's what he thought every time he went in. She wanted to be at home with them, not in some hospital. She bad-mouthed hospitals, she and Arthur Gillies. No, she wanted to die at home, in her own bed, with her family around her. Late afternoon her room got the light, and when she was dying she wanted the sun, to feel it on her skin and in her eyes.

Her breathing had slowed in the days before she died as she began to wind down. Her voice was faint – he drew in to hear and her rotten breath made him want to retch. She was barely there. Her hand was cool, too cool, but it moved; the fingers dialled patterns on the sheets. Not motherless, not yet, but close. Then, thinking there was time, he left the room. He made himself a cup of tea, ate four or five biscuits. He couldn't say why he fiddled with the broken larder latch, as if he were going to mend it, for it had been broken for years; why he watched *Home and Away* – it wasn't a soap he watched. Mama died before the credits rolled. She died alone. The paramedics said it was often the way. They didn't know why, except that animals did it: they died alone, at peace with themselves.

Is that what it was? Peace? Is that what happened at the end, when the body came off like a shirt over the head?

When Mama lay in her coffin, her hair looked just right: a wig as black as vinyl, the kind they made records from. London's own Bettie Page. They had sat up all night with the body, Rita and Annetta, drinking sweet sherry and toasting our Sal. They changed her clothes until they were satisfied, primping her with make-up and jewellery, the wig in pride of place.

Her hair, Joseph thought, when he joined them in the morning, looked like burnt spun sugar on a white paper cone. The cancer had stripped her body of flesh and her bright waxy mouth seemed to scream out of her skull.

She looked, he thought, like a strumpet.

Funny how when Joseph was a boy, she didn't look like that to him, with her face always painted, dressed up. His mother and her friends cared for him tenderly and faithfully, even if they cooked the Sunday lunch in low-cut spangled gowns or stood to attention when the doorbell rang halfway through the meal, baring their shoulders of the woolly cardigans they wore to keep warm when customers weren't in the house. He didn't know they were different; he had no friends, hadn't met other mothers.

But in death, Joseph didn't want her to look like that, not after all they'd been through the last few years. First the cancer diagnosis: her lungs, just like her father and uncles and brothers, the pit workers; a plague among them. With treatment, the cancer went away. Everyone celebrated but no one was surprised, for Mama was a tough nut. Almost a year passed while it grew invisibly again. One day it was blue skies and then the sun dropped out of sight: cancer, cancer, everywhere. Cancer in her bones, her brain, her liver, hungrier than ever, starved of her flesh during those long months of cure and ready to gorge. So many men had said, 'I could eat you whole, you sweet thing,' when she was young and beautiful, and so she said, surfacing from her sedation, that the cancer was for her sins. 'We stand before God stripped of our worldly possessions. We stand in His judgement.' God would have her brilliant hair, her cleavage, her dense, grey gaze, the roses of her complexion, her hot, deep mouth. She would stand before Him in her bones, she whispered, extending to Joseph a wasted arm that rattled its bracelets.

'What about me? What will happen to me?'

'You stay here.' It was all arranged; Mr Wye had seen to things. They had often spoken of it, she said, over tea. She was certain of the arrangement. Joseph had nothing to fear: the house was his, or when Mama died it was. She promised. It was her way of looking after him even when she was gone.

He left Mama's room and went upstairs. Annetta's door was open. He looked in. All her clothes and possessions appeared to be piled on the bed: a dun-coloured dome-shaped load. *Chewed*-looking. He poked the nest and it collapsed. She was not there. He went downstairs to the kitchen, where he had last seen her. Not there. The drawing room, her chair, then all the other rooms, up and down the stairs, double-checking – he even peered out into the garden. She was not anywhere. He was breathless with looking. She was gone. For the second time that day she was gone.

6

On Monday morning Marie went back to work and Flavia cleaned Marie's bedroom. Flavia had her rota around the house, her weekly routine, and Monday was bedrooms and bed linen, when she washed and ironed their sheets. She couldn't resist a peek in Marie's drawers when she dusted, just to see the state of them. She felt under the mattress for sweet wrappers and had a good look inside the wardrobe – just to see.

She was always happy to have the house to herself again. She needed to restore order, for no matter how tidy Marie tried to be – and she did try, bless her – she still disturbed the surfaces. She tracked in dirt. She shed hairs; she filed her nails into piles of powder. She left fingerprints. She slopped her tea, drips that dried into just a bit of colour, and she had a habit of leaving teaspoons in unexpected places: on the mantelpiece, the hall table, next to the bathroom sink. Flavia collected the teaspoons and soaped them till they shone and she never said a word about it to Marie.

Housework lifted Flavia's spirits. She could see a result.

If she felt low, she emptied out a cupboard or scrubbed the hob. Flavia cleaned the old-fashioned way and it took time, but time was what she had, bags of it, and she was not given to putting her feet up in front of the telly the way some women did the minute they'd scrambled the beds together, leaving the dishes dripping soapsuds in a rack over the sink. Not Flavia. She dried her dishes and put them away where they belonged. Everything had a place. She ironed her tea towels – she ironed every scrap that came out of her washing machine. She didn't use the same cloth on everything.

There. Just the hoovering to do and she did it properly, using all the attachments. It felt honest, keeping things tidy. Nothing to hide. Flavia knew her house inside out and she brightened the corners rain or shine. It was something to do and it passed the time, but more than that, it was a deep feeling, a *fervour* in her. God gave her hands to clean.

Marie didn't mind Flavia doing her room – if anything, she was grateful. But she did hide things. Nail varnish in every bright colour. Perfume, expensive-looking bottles, all of them unopened. Make-up still in its wrapping. Face creams, eye creams, tubes of this, pots of that, sample sachets, none of it to stay. Things appeared and were gone and more would come. Flavia rifled expertly and never peeped. She didn't know why Marie bought those things.

Her stomach rumbled. She thought about lunch: chicken soup with rice. A glance at the kitchen clock showed her there was still an hour and a half to go before she could eat. She took a skewer, the kind she used for meat kebabs and baking potatoes, and wrapped a bit of rag around the tip before setting to work on the hard-to-reach places: the crease where the window frame met its pane, the long sticky crevice between the cooker and worktop. That's what she did when she had the time. If the clock still was not showing right, she re-sewed buttons that never stood a chance of dropping off. It was the path she chose in life. She got herself moving, pulled herself forward, went up and down the stairs, putting things away where they belonged. She tried not to think. She prayed instead. Prayer, like housework, kept Flavia busy all day.

*

Marie watched the raindrops slip down the street window of the Linen Cupboard, their race so unpredictable and utterly absorbing. There were no customers because of the downpour – a rare afternoon of bad weather, after weeks of heatwave, and she was grateful for a quiet day. Mrs Albright, the owner, was in the back. Marie had a cup of tea and a biscuit and she perched herself in such a way so as to have a bit of privacy.

She had been to see Mr Wye again. He was less guarded with every meeting – he even seemed to want to help. He had known her father in the army; the war threw them together, unlikely friends, better at business. Arthur had looked him up not long after he started in property, around the time Marie was born, and they had worked together until his death. He said she reminded him of her father. The killer instinct, Mr Wye called it.

Her father, apparently, had been a shrewd businessman, seizing opportunity over and over again. She had seen the list of the properties he owned: twenty houses in Mayfair, Chelsea, Soho, Westminster, Regent's Park and Primrose Hill. London was having a property boom such as never before and Mr Wye assured her that her father had predicted it years ago. Arthur Gillies believed that London was a miraculous city, possessing nine lives, for no matter how many times the city almost perished, it always triumphed; rebuilt and got rid of the rats.

'If only your father had that kind of right to life,' Mr Wye said, and bowed his head.

Marie had been at work when her father died. Flavia kept the policeman waiting outside. He could surely see her peering out at him from a window, but she wouldn't answer the bell. Marie found the policeman on the front step when she returned home at half five. He was smoking a cigarette – a dozen more were stubbed out in a neat pile by his left foot. A neighbour had offered him a cup of tea. Everyone knew it was bad news.

Marie had never seen a man so bald as that officer. No eyebrows or lashes, not a trace of a beard. As she listened to him she stared. Then she put her key in the door and opened it to find Flavia right there – she fell into Marie's arms, shaking uncontrollably. She knew without anyone telling her. Flavia asked Marie to help her to bed, and as she went downstairs Marie heard her howl.

Marie invited the policeman to stay a while. He declined;

he had been a long time waiting there. She hadn't seen a wedding ring on his finger, but that didn't mean anything.

'Cup of tea?'

'I better be off,' he said. He shook her hand. 'I'm sorry for your loss.'

Marie did not cry. She heard Flavia sobbing upstairs and it tore at her but she didn't cry. Later, eyes still dry, she stood buttering some bread for her tea when a magpie appeared at the kitchen window. The magpie tapped on the pane with his beak, regarding her with tinsel eyes. Behind him, the evening sky had been raked into streaks of orange and pink. The magpie tapped the glass again. He tapped and tapped. It was her father, Marie realized. He tapped as if he would like to come in. He cocked his little head. His eyes burned brightly. Her hand went up – did she shoo him away or did he just fly off?

I am Marie Gillies. I am forty-one years old. My father has died. A cry snarled in her throat but did not bite. What would it take to cry?

It took weeks. They said she was stoic. At the small funeral, draped in black from head to toe, Marie did not weep. Her mother sat with one hand on the coffin through-out the service; she overflowed with grief, drenching her funeral veil. When they gathered at the graveside, Marie feared Flavia would climb into the hole and so increased her grip: a conduit to Flavia's endless sorrow. But even watching the coffin drop and the dirt shovelled in heavy wet spadefuls didn't do the trick, nor did seeing the empty hearse drive off, and their car, too, when Flavia could bear it, leaving her father behind.

Marie looked over old photographs. She dredged up memories of Christmas. She held the gold wristwatch her father had given her on her eighteenth birthday, listening to it tick, a heart in her hand. She had always hated him, and loved him, too, because they went together, those two. She might have married, just to get away from him, but then she could never bring herself to leave her mother, for she was all her mother had in the world, apart from her father – and now he was gone.

Mrs Albright came to the front of the shop where Marie was watching the rain. 'When you've finished,' she said, 'there are beach towels to be unpacked.' It was June, coming up to holiday season, when shoppers would be tempted to buy such things. Marie nodded and smiled to herself, thinking of her own trip. She might buy a beach towel. There were beaches in Italy.

Mrs Albright left her to it. When she was good and ready, Marie went to rinse out her mug. As she passed the counter, she heard Kelly saying something about Marie's tea break being longer than what the others had. 'Me, if I'm five minutes in the loo, it's "Kelly, I'm docking you."' Kelly raised her voice, as if Marie couldn't hear. 'Look at that, she's eating on the floor. It ain't allowed but she'll get away with it, just you see.'

It wasn't the first time Kelly had spoken out like that. Marie swallowed the last bite of her biscuit and looked at the girl, a big girl like Marie had been – but she would never have dared stuff herself into the short skirts and tiny tops that Kelly favoured. Marie had been bred with a kind of gentility. As a child she wore ribbons in her dark hair and woollen vests year-round, knitted by Flavia herself. Always immaculate, her fingernails clipped short and the dirt scraped out of them – not that she spent much time playing outdoors. Her mother didn't encourage it.

'You dropped crumbs, Marie.' Kelly's tone was aggressive. She had no place in the shop, a girl like that.

Marie squared up to her. 'This isn't the estate,' she said. She didn't know where it came from. She thought there was something wrong with her blood pressure. She felt as if she might explode.

The bell on the shop door went. Kelly ducked behind the counter and disappeared from view. The customer, dressed in pastel flowers, looked at Marie, smiling expectantly. Marie put down her mug, right next to the cash register, just above Kelly's head. No mugs on the counter was the rule. Go to the customer immediately was another. Marie turned her back on the customer and headed for the rear of the shop, where her things were. She put on her mac, took up her handbag and sailed out of the front door without saying a word to anyone.

*

Pater noster, qui es in caelis, sanctificetur nomen tuum. Flavia closed the door to Marie's room. She went downstairs and tidied away the cleaning things, then got into position on the kitchen lino, rocking from side to side to give her knees some relief. Prayer was as bad as scrubbing floors sometimes.

She prayed for Marie's soul, among other things. Marie had always been a good girl, but she hadn't been properly baptized. Arthur was an atheist. He didn't like anything that got in his way, including God. He thought Flavia was a fool for having faith. So, one afternoon, when Arthur was away in London, Flavia put Marie in a bath she had anointed with holy water from a local Catholic church, and prayed over her baby, following the baptism rite from a borrowed hymnal. She hoped it was enough – she'd been worrying all this time. Pray with me, she sometimes wanted to call to the world – she would open the windows and shout so that all could hear – to keep my daughter safe and get her into heaven.

The same prayer every day, and today she tacked on a Glory Be.

Up she got. Looked out of the window: abundant grey, stuffed with cloud, a sky about to rain again. Time to start the washing – she had whites to brighten, and tonight it would be crisp sheets reeking of detergent and starch when she laid her soul to sleep.

*

Marie couldn't believe what she'd done. The look on their faces! *Marie.* She wasn't one to surprise, always so quiet. Did her job and did it right. Of all people!

A dark horse, Mrs Albright muttered, unpacking the beach towels herself.

Marie found herself on the pavement, walking briskly in the rain. Just walking. Gulps of air. Stopping with the lights and then going great guns again – it didn't matter where she went. She was free, for a bit. Until five o'clock, at least, and then she must get home or Flavia would worry and call the shop – that's what she had done ten years ago, the only other time Marie was late from work, having stopped off at WH Smith to do some Christmas shopping. She simply lost track of time in the gaiety of extra lights and sparkly decorations and carols piped from above, choosing presents for her colleagues. Flavia was beside herself when Marie arrived just twenty minutes later than usual – not long, but clearly a hellish delay for Flavia, who remained anguished for a few days. What could have been: Flavia lived *that*, the other version, what didn't happen. Marie wasn't sure Flavia had ever let it go, even now, ten years on.

A stitch in her side from all the walking – she had better sit. She found a bus shelter; nice to get out of the rain, and no one else was using it. Marie was alone. She could think.

It was the money that made her do it: knowing she had money in the bank fortified her in some way. She didn't feel afraid; she felt strong. She was going to have a new life. She would have to arrange an increase in allowance with Mr Wye and Mr Dagger-Davis and she knew she could do that now.

But Flavia – what would she tell Flavia? So many questions would come of telling, and Marie didn't have the answers herself yet. If Flavia knew that she had quit, she would panic: the loss of income, no matter how it was spent, for Marie contributed to their household budget and always had done, as arranged by her father long ago. If she told Flavia one thing, she would have to tell her everything else, too.

It was time to go home. Marie was undecided the whole way, right until she walked through the door.

'Ma?'

She didn't have to ask: Marie knew where Flavia was and what she was doing, knew from the windows misted over and the fact of it being Monday: Flavia was ironing bed sheets. She would be finishing up, the kitchen full of steam, the surfaces and Flavia herself dripping. Their supper would be all but ready to eat.

Marie put the ironing board away under the stairs while her mother set the iron to cool in a corner. Flavia washed and dried her hands. Marie laid the table. Flavia filled their plates, made the tea. They sat and faced each other.

'So,' Flavia said.

'Yes?' Marie answered, somewhat anxiously.

'How was your day?'

'Fine. The same,' Marie said. 'It rained, so it was slow.' The thing that was inside her now did not come out and show itself.

7

Rita was having the time of her life, so she kept saying. Edward poured the wine, ordered a second bottle. They drank it. When the bill arrived and he had paid, he put his hand over hers. 'What do you say we move on? I know a little place.' She didn't even blink.

On the walk to the hotel, he put his arm around her proprietorially. Rita liked it when a man did that: she wanted to be owned – paid for and taken home. She remembered a time when she had accounts all over town in every fine store, and flats for which she didn't pay the rent, ready-furnished, not another woman's hairpin in sight, nothing for her to do except be there, waiting, ready, purring like a pretty pussycat.

She leaned into Edward, trying not to wobble as they walked. Legs like jelly. Edward was saying something she didn't quite catch. She threw back her head and laughed. How was it that she didn't know where they were? Rita knew Soho like the back of her hand. She stumbled, grabbed at him: he was solid, capable, and she felt the strength in his arm, to keep her afloat. He was almost eighty but his arm was a young man's arm.

'Steady on now,' he said.

They passed a girl half obscured in the shadows of a stairwell; she shivered in the shortest of summer dresses and her bare skin prickled. The days were hot but the nights were cold, for as soon as the sun went down the temperature plummeted. She wanted a coat, the lamb. She clutched a teddy bear. Rita, the drink in her making her sweet, smiled at the girl, swelling with feeling. They were the same person, she and the girl. The girl curled her lip. She called after them, 'Come see me later, Grandpa. Tuck me in.'

Not tonight, Rita thought. Tonight the air sang for Rita Sourbeer. Edward seemed not to have noticed the girl, determined as he was on their hotel. His feet chopped at the pavement in good leather shoes; he marched, keeping a firm grip on Rita. She talked for two. What did he think of the new vista? The Gherkin, she meant. Seemed a silly thing to build, *she* thought, sticking up in the middle of things like that. Like a you-know-what. She laughed. He didn't reply, just looked straight ahead and kept walking. None of the new buildings made sense to her, she continued. They looked like petrol stations, most of them. Who wanted to live in a petrol station? What she liked was comfy, warm rooms. Square rooms, painted yellow.

'I love a yellow room. What you want is a friendly yellow room to beat all this grey weather we have in England. If I were rich I'd get away every winter and go somewhere sunny. When I married my third husband, we went to

Turkey and it was pure heaven, I tell you. Pure bliss. All them beaches and nothing to do but lie around.' Rita was off, remembering. They went out on a boat, she said, but the sea was rough and Paul – her third husband, she was sure about that – he went green around the gills with seasickness, and then *she* was sick, just from thinking about it too much. 'You can talk yourself into anything,' she said. 'Any fine mess.'

Edward grunted. She hummed a few bars of 'Tampico'. Did he know it? Stan Kenton and June Christy. 'I used to be crazy about "Tampico". We listened to it constantly. All night long. All day and all night. We wore the record out.'

'Here we are,' he said, stopping suddenly.

Rita looked around – the gaudy lights, the latrine stink of the narrow street. There was broken glass under foot. That was Soho for you. It never changed. Even with the new shops and clubs and restaurants, all of them upmarket places, it was still a dirty cave. Piss in the puddles, scraps of rotten sandwich sleeting the cobbles. Always something on your shoe in Soho, and the feeling of someone's eyes following you – Rita looked over her shoulder as they went in.

They checked into the hotel as man and wife. Edward counted out some notes and handed them over. Rita smiled at the receptionist. What was the harm in what they were doing? Two adults having a bit of fun, nothing wrong with that. They went up in the lift, Edward quiet, not looking at her. Did he know there were hidden cameras in every lift? There were cameras everywhere and people sat in front of tellies in big office buildings, watching the whole of London,

Rita told him. Did he know that? It was all the crime, proper murders with knives, and carjacking. Had he read about carjacking? Terrifying. She had never learned to drive. There was no need to in London. She could go anywhere she wanted on public transport. She could take the Green Line if she wanted some fresh air. The lift stopped at the fourth floor. The doors opened. Down the hall they went, up to their ears in carpet, Rita chattering all the way. She liked the look of the hotel, she said. Businesslike. She was sure a lot of businessmen used it. Edward expertly swiped the key card and they were in.

'Isn't this nice? A yellow room. I do love a yellow room. How perfect. How charming,' Rita said, and really, she was delighted.

The line of his mouth softened at last. 'I'll just be a moment,' he said, locking the door to the bathroom.

She drew the curtains, feeling the weight of the gold brocade. Very nice. She hung up her coat and turned before the mirror, fluffing her curls. She re-touched her lipstick and eyebrows. No sign of Edward. She sat on the bed to wait, crossing her legs. She inspected her nails, nipping the cuticles with her front teeth. *Tidying*. A woman's hands said it all. Rita always wore rubber gloves when she did the washing-up, and she varnished her nails red every Sunday evening, when she packed her face in mud and sipped sweet sherry through a straw.

A long time passed. Rita still smiled but she began to feel a bit of hollowness somewhere deep inside her. It wouldn't go wrong now, she told herself. He was just having a wash, and then it would be her turn to wash and she would go to him like a vision in expensive black knickers and bra, high heels on to make her legs look long. She still depilated, she shaved and plucked and oiled herself from head to toe. She would twirl and ask him, did he like her now? They never said no. Once she had him in bed he would never want to leave. She took hold of her knee to stop it jigging. What she needed was a drink. She helped herself to the minibar: a glug of gin, a splash of tonic. She drank it down like sunshine and lay back on the bed. Yes, that was better. The overhead lights made her squint. She closed her eyes. The sound of running water relaxed her no end. He splashed like a baby in the bath; Rita smiled to herself to hear it.

When she woke she didn't know where she was. The yellow walls – not hers. The smell of strong disinfectant, the patterned carpet showing stains, the bedspread on which she lay, creasing her dress; none of it was hers. She wiped her chin and sat up, caught a glimpse of herself in the mirror: her flattened curls, a loose look to her mouth, the hump in her back showing. She reached for the glass on the bedside table, drank the nothing that was in it – she felt a fool for doing that. The minibar, she thought. Any old thing would do. Get it down. Then she knocked at the bathroom door.

'William?'

There was no reply.

She knocked again, harder. 'William?' She tried the door handle, which was locked. 'William, open the door before I call for help.'

The door suddenly swung wide and a gentleman appeared, red-faced, his trousers gathered about his waist in one hand. 'What's all the racket? What are you on about?'

'William, I thought – I thought you were ill, or had fallen, or – something.'

He made an incredulous gesture. 'I was taking my bloody Viagra.'

Of course he was. Viagra was all the rage. 'Well.' She smiled at him, flapped her false eyelashes.

'Who's this William, anyway? My name is Edward!' He shut the door.

Rita blinked. Edward? Oh yes. *Lunch.*

*

She had been doing it long enough to know when the moment was coming. It came. Never a surprise, after all that shoving. First there was the tussle with her brassiere – she wanted it left on. She insisted. It cost her a pretty penny and held everything together. Her other bits she didn't half mind in their collapse, but her bosom needed lifting if she wanted to be the fantasy.

Then a bit of spanking. She whispered, lots of whispering; filthy things to spur him on, nonsense, really. She got the raisin of his withered earlobe in her mouth and nibbled. The tufts of hair that burst from the ear itself tickled her nose. She moved on to the fine mesh at the back of his neck; she covered every inch of his trunk with her hands, smoothing things out. He licked his lips. When he'd had enough of all that, he turned her over and the bed began to shake.

It could go on and on, the engulfment, the *occupation*, especially when Viagra had been taken.

It took an hour with Viagra, at least.

She heard another room's shower running. She heard the television, not theirs. She heard the lift ping. When he twisted her round like that her eyes overflowed. Her old bones did sometimes feel as if they would break. He never looked at her. He kept his eyes closed and his face raised as if to praise the heavens, as if to call down an angel and place her beneath him instead.

It was just sex – she could bear it. Rita knew when an affair wasn't going anywhere. Dinner and a room. Well. A nice little earner, she told herself.

He cried out and was done. 'Thanks,' he muttered. A quick nap with his back to her, snoring heartily, and then he returned to the bathroom where she could hear him washing again. He soon emerged, fully dressed except for his tie, which bulged in his breast pocket.

'Oh,' he said. 'You're still here.'

She had been thinking of what she would spend the money on. Her heating bill, first off, and there might be something left over for her to treat herself. She had no doubt that he would pay; he'd been generous with the dinner tip, and she provided a good service, if she did say so herself. Plenty of conversation, all of it cheery stuff, nothing about death. She stayed off the subject of death as best she could: nobody wanted to talk about that. She never ordered the steak unless she was sure of her companion's deep pockets. One never knew with pensioners. Oh, she liked a drink or two, but who didn't? They were out enjoying themselves. They'd worked hard all their lives, hadn't they? Hadn't they just.

And in the bedroom, well. *Well*.

'Fancy a drink?' she said.

'I better be getting on for home. It's gone midnight.' He took out his wallet and, without looking at her, laid some notes on the bedside table. She counted with him: one hundred. 'Be a good girl now and get yourself ready to go.'

'We've got the room for the night, haven't we? Seems a shame not to put it to use.' Rita patted the bed. She liked Edward. She didn't want him to get away. She couldn't be sure that she would have another chance with him if he left, and she wasn't the kind to chase a man. She was old-fashioned like that – her generation, she always said.

He cleared his throat. 'You're welcome to stay. The room is paid for.'

That's not what she meant at all. He was slippery, this one. She heard her voice, light and easy. She was clever like that. 'I had a lovely time, Edward.'

'Goodnight.'

'Goodnight.'

The door closed. She listened for the lift. She waited for him to ride down, exit and nod – or not – at the sleepy receptionist on his way out. When she was sure that he was quite gone, she emptied the contents of the minibar into her handbag.

Rita used to work in hotels and so she knew her way out of one, the quietest way, the way to leave without being seen, except, of course, on CCTV. Not the lift, but the stairs, which no one ever used, except for the maids, and which needed paint and were badly lit and smelled of drains. Rita hurried as best she could – she had been a zippy thing in her day. She didn't mind stairs. She carried her shoes. She prayed she wouldn't meet a soul, for she wasn't decent under her coat, plus she had the minibar clanking away in her handbag, and then there was the question of what she was doing on the stairs in the first place, clearly leaving the wrong way when there was a perfectly good lift and front entrance to the hotel.

She made it. The fire door slammed hard behind her and she jumped, oh lord, how she jumped! Rita put her hand to her heart. Then she slipped on her shoes and stepped to the kerb to hail a taxi.

*

A dog was following, a stray – if such a thing still existed in the centre of London in the twenty-first century. They were a couple of strays, he and she, identities unknown: one a barker, the other human but without the means to communicate.

They were looking for the den. Annetta remembered it being somewhere in the park. They searched a long time, and then, something familiar. The dog knew it too, running ahead of her, on the scent, tail erect. He marked at the den's entrance and disappeared inside. She followed him, inhaling the musk. A fox had been there.

Church bells tolled. Her feet were heavy with mud. She stroked the bit of bacon she'd brought, the rasher warm as a hand. She held it.

The sound of a door closing. She was deep inside herself. She took nothing with her, not even her clothes. She was so cold. She jiggled herself, arms crossed over her chest, flattening her breasts – her breasts that were already hanging flat. The dog lay down next to her. Where she was, it was dark, still, not exactly quiet: there were the usual sounds of a distant world – cars, sirens, trains running north, blaring their horns to clear the tracks. She rocked. She comforted herself like that. The dog whined and smacked his chops. He was after the bacon in her fist. He licked her hand, nosed the fingers open. She snapped them shut. He lay down, whimpered, eyes appealing. He put his teeth around her hand and the pain of it startled her into being. Sometimes she caught hold of herself and knew it was her mind going. Worse than cancer, this death. Cancer you could treat – you could kill it, or if it killed you, it killed fast. Fast enough. But not what she had. It killed slow, dementia did, burying her inch by inch. She was already in above her neck.

The dog. She panted. After a while she didn't feel the teeth going in.

At first they were just voices, anyone's voices, much of a muchness. Then they were calling her: Annetta. Annetta! *Ann!* At least she knew that was her name. Her name was in the deepest part of her mind, near the beginning. As near to the beginning as she could get.

*

Oh, she got cross, Rita did. Every little thing set her off. His mother always said there was as much good in Rita as any other person, but he had his doubts. Bruised fruit, bad manners, dogs off the lead, bike couriers speeding past, knocking everyone off their feet – but nothing made her angrier than Annetta disappearing, and lately Annetta was always disappearing.

At first, when Annetta's dementia was beginning to show, she never wanted to be alone. Joseph minded that. He felt under siege. Everywhere he went, she followed, pestering him with questions, always the same questions: would it rain? Were the buses running to schedule? Where were her spectacles? Once or twice he had enough and really lost it: just bellowing. It was wrong to shout at someone who cowered and hid her face, who didn't understand – who didn't know what she was doing to make him so mad. Rita said she didn't blame him. Annetta would test the patience of a saint, Rita said. But he loved Annetta. She had always been his favourite – from the moment she appeared at the house in the Crescent when he was two years old, according to Sal. He didn't remember the other girls who lived in the house before Rita and Annetta, but he knew their names: Minnie, Louise, Ava, Charlie, Dot. None of them had lasted long. Rita and Annetta arrived together and never left. They all stayed put after that. Mama called them her family.

Annetta was so pretty when she was young, pink and white and golden, a proper dolly with a tinkling laugh. She loved to laugh. She favoured blue to set off her eyes. Her hands were small and soft and dimpled, like his own when he was a boy – he held her hand to keep her captive by his side. And he was her darling, better than any man, Annetta said. Joseph was meant to stay upstairs in his nursery, but he did sometimes creep down, and when he saw Annetta going off on the arm of one gentleman or another he was always crushed. *Jealous.* Given a chance, he would have had a go at those men, tied up their shoelaces so they tripped and fell to their deaths down the stairs, or stolen their wallets. That was before he understood what went on in the bedrooms – and when he did understand, when he was old enough to know, he hated those men all the more. If Annetta guessed his thoughts, she never said, but she was careful not to let him see her fully undressed.

Now he saw her naked all the time: the shrunken breasts, the flesh that hung. Her glorious yellow hair had thinned and greyed and been cropped, her blue eyes dimmed with cataracts, her pretty hands buckled and spotted – hands that clutched at him and made him think of chicken feet, of which he had always been frightened.

He stood at the front window, looking out, seeking her apparition in the dusk. He willed her to emerge from the shadows of the park. She did not come. How he *lived* Annetta's death sometimes and felt, in those moments, bereft.

She was another mother, now that his mother was dead. She had only ever been kind to him. She kept her handbag stocked with sweets and let him dig; she wasn't one of those, like Rita, who guarded her handbag and would never let anyone see what was inside. Annetta had doted on him. It was only since she became ill that she didn't. Now she didn't even know who he was.

Joseph went to the phone and dialled. He had been calling Rita for hours. He let it ring on and on. He had never been in Rita's flat, so had no picture of her telephone ringing off the hook. Here, they had just the one phone in the front hall, next to the coat stand. Its ring was shrill, old-fashioned; it sliced the air into pieces when it rang, but it rarely rang. Only a few times a year, at most, and those were mostly wrong numbers.

Back to the front window. Sweat poured from him, soaking his shirt. His breathing was ragged, despite using his inhaler. Not now, he thought. Not that now. Joseph had had asthma all his life. He tried to bear it, to live as others did, walking, climbing the stairs, but it left him breathless. He couldn't go chasing after Annetta; his lungs would riot. He would never find her on his own. He wasn't good at things like that. Besides, it was important that he should be at home if she returned, to open the door. She wouldn't have taken a key with her.

He gazed at the park across the way, not beckoning, just there. The *maze* of it. What Annetta went looking for, he didn't know, but every time she was found hiding in a bush. Never the same bush.

He dialled Rita again, idly fishing among the coats that hung nearby as he did: Annetta's blue mac, bits of tissue foaming from the pockets, and his own trench, handed down from Arthur Gillies; other assorted cardigans, scarves, Mama's shabby silver fox buried at the bottom. Joseph stroked the fur, swirling its worn pile. If only Mama were here. Mama would never have let Annetta slip out of the front door like that. Mama always knew just what to do, and she wasn't above a good slap, either, to keep her girls in line.

He tried Rita: no answer. He was so alone. He went to the window. Across the way, the park entrance loomed, a mouth that swallowed people. His chest tightened, the breath snicked out. With some effort now, he got to the phone. He dialled, listened a long time, put it down.

*

She was up again.

There was somewhere else to go. Another place, more sacred. Annetta scattered gravel in her determination to get there. Her shoes were boots like she used to wear, leather trotters that pinched her feet, worn by her sister first; not a comfortable pair. Her cardigan (she felt it round her shoulders) had belonged to her cousin; her hat, there on top of her head, the one with the chewed brim, came from a neighbour. Nothing was new to her, not even her underwear, which had seen better days.

A dog on her heels – that's how it always was. Outside of town, blue hills in the distance, the smell of wood fires. Tall grasses tickled her chin; nettles she barely touched, just caught the sting of; docks, ferns, feathery evergreens. She swung a catkin like a noisemaker as she ran from the tramps who walked the roads, abominably drunk. Come 'ere, they called to her. Give 'em something they wanted, the makings of a cigarette, or a kiss. She cursed them and they laughed. She was only little.

There. She dropped to her knees and scrabbled inward, in the dirt. And then—

How long? She never knew. It was like being underwater: time went funny.

She heard a voice – someone touched her, a smear of human warmth.

She pushed and pinched. She fought. She spat, liking that. She pulled hair. She was just getting going and then she opened her eyes. The dog was gone. Annetta scrambled to her feet. She managed to curtsey. She had lost her hat again – not in her hand when she scraped the ground. She toppled and landed on her backside. Her mother would be cross. It was the neighbour's hat, not hers. Hats went around like that. What was a hat? A hat was to keep the rain off.

Twigs in her hair, mud in the creases and folds of her old skin. Annetta lay back and closed her eyes – as though if she didn't look at them, didn't answer their questions, they weren't really there. Their uniforms gave her the creeps. No one liked a copper where she came from.

With her eyes closed, she was in another place.

It took a long time. They used everything they could think of, every trick, entreating her with smiles before directing her, in stern voices, to get a move on. They would carry her out of there, they warned. There was something off-putting about Annetta. Her nudity, for one thing, but it wasn't that. She was crude in her bearing, the way her legs drew wide. She spreadeagled and showed herself to them.

The dog had returned and paced menacingly just beyond the lamplight. Annetta, seeing the brutish stray, cried out, 'There you are, my darling!' The dog ran to her and began to lick: her feet, her dirty knees and thighs. Annetta rolled with the dog's thrusting nose.

'Get that fucking dog out of here,' one of the officers said.

The dog licked Annetta's hand, kissed it fervently, unable to stop, and they saw the closed fist was raw, bleeding. 'It wants me,' she said.

'What do you have there? What's in your hand?'

'Nothing.' But she began to cry with the pain.

'Open your hand. Let him have it, whatever it is.'

Her fist opened. The bacon rasher dropped out. The dog snatched it up and ran off. Annetta wept, cradling her hand.

'What was it?'

'It was mine.'

'But what was it?'

Annetta did not, would not say. She would be led, however, and they left the park.

*

Rita drew the curtains before she switched on the lights. She put them all on, every single one, and set the kettle to boil for a hot-water bottle. She had left her torn blouse and stockings in the hotel bathroom bin. Just like a public-school boy to be so clumsy and rough, she thought. Long years of marriage did not make them expert lovers; widowhood made matters worse, for they took it when they could get it and they needed it too much.

Rita unloaded the minibar from her handbag and, after lining up the little bottles, selected Teacher's. She drank it neat. She listened to the church bells strike one. Another drink – Absolut vodka. Like paint thinner. Give her a glass of sweet sherry anytime.

Well. It was nice to just sit for a minute. Wasn't it nice? Another nip of something and then she'd go and have a wash – the old routine after a date, to keep the waterworks functioning properly.

Rita thought it had gone well. It was coming back to her now. Dinner was pleasant enough, with few of those sticky silences she hated. When a man wasn't talking, that meant things weren't on.

She tried to remember what she had eaten with Edward. She remembered the first course, a bowl of red pepper soup that gave her the burps, but then what? She poured herself a sweet sherry – at last, a proper drink. She drained the glass and poured another.

Lamb, was it? Rump? She would remember fussing over a bird: all the bitty parts. Funny that she couldn't remember – she had a memory like flypaper. She remembered, for instance, that Walter, another one that got away, wore mismatched socks. That's how she knew he wasn't married.

They always said they weren't, but half of them were. Edward was a widower. Poor Edward, but then he hadn't liked her much.

Well.

There was one man who bent right over his food and shovelled it in as quick as he could, then sat back and asked her if she wouldn't mind skipping pudding, he would get the bill and they could be off. But Rita loved to chat, which made her a slow eater, and she had a sweet tooth, too, so they had to see pudding through. She chewed every mouthful until there was nothing left to chew. She sipped her wine more delicately than usual. She ordered a molten chocolate pudding that took twenty minutes to cook. When they finally fell into bed, he was pure disappointment, chasing his pleasure with no thought as to how she might be getting on. Then he got her in his arms and tightened his hold as if he would never let go – he was one of those. A clutcher. It was beyond human endurance sometimes, agony to her bones.

There was another, Peter, whose wife had dementia. Bridie, the wife was called. Once a month Peter checked Bridie into respite care and went and found a woman who could see to his needs. For a while, he and Rita had an arrangement, but then he said that after fifty years of marriage he fancied a variety. She heard from him again a few years later, after his wife died. He wanted to thank her, he said. He had a new wife already, someone he met in the sheltered accommodation where he and Bridie had eventually retired. He said, laughing, that the place was full of swingers and they were all having the time of their lives. He thought Rita would do good business there.

She felt no shame in what she did. Years ago, when she was living in the house in the Crescent with Sal and Annetta, a woman had turned up at the door in tears, wanting to know what it was all about, why her husband was there. Rita had sat her down and explained that it was nothing to do with love, it was a *service* they provided. That's what Sal always called it: a service. The best service in town. She made the business of sex sound practical.

Well. So it was. Practical, that is. Rita always had money in her purse. She earned her own keep, and it was easy enough: undress, lie down. One breast in the mouth, then the other. A lewd conversation: you are this, you are that. Beautiful. Sexy. Soft. Smell so good. And you. Big. Hard. Fat. Old. Rich, or rich enough. Sometimes missing bits – fingers, toes, testicles, or an eye – there, put it there, a water glass next to the lamp. I don't mind, she said. I want you, they said. Who were they? Who did they think they were? What did Rita care? Men needed her. They spoke to her of their longing, their desire, the ache in them. She had the power. Men wanted her to want them and they believed that she did. They believed her when she said she did and she said – she said anything. Just to keep it going.

One more wee drink, what was the harm in it? And after such a night, too. Go on, she told herself. Have another one. Who was to say she shouldn't? At her age! A drop of what she fancied wasn't likely to kill her.

She must have fallen asleep in her chair, for there she was

when the phone rang at half one in the morning. Who could it be, at that hour? Who phoned so late at night except a lover, or an ex-lover – or a crank? Maybe it was Edward. If he wanted to chat, she would explain that she needed her beauty sleep but they could always meet up for lunch. That was proper. That was the way forward with a man. If he wanted a quickie that late at night – she had heard it all before – she would tell him no. Lunch, she'd insist, and get it in the diary.

'Hello?'

Joseph stammered something – she didn't catch what he said, but she'd know his stutter anywhere.

'What?' Rita blinked. 'Oh, for goodness' sake, it's the middle of the night! What are you like? I told you to watch her!' She slammed down the phone so hard she cracked the receiver.

*

Rita met Joseph's protests that he had been looking after Annetta with a tight mouth. 'How long has she been gone?'

He didn't know. He couldn't say. It had taken him hours to reach Rita and he was exhausted from his efforts. He let his head droop onto his chest and roll there. 'Don't look pathetic,' she said. She asked him for a torch. 'You're coming with me.'

He balked. Shook his head. He was tired. Rita snapped at him – he got his coat.

The park was not locked. They just walked in, calling for

Annetta, searching the shrubbery and undergrowth, the light of their torch not showing much. Rita cursed Joseph and Annetta alternately. 'She can die out here, for all I care, running off at this hour. And you—' She pointed a quivering finger at him. 'It will be on your head.'

They looked everywhere, travelling all the paths. Joseph's feet ached from walking. The moon waned. There were fewer cars and just a handful of lit windows in the houses and flats around the park. It was so late. Rita finally hailed a passing taxi, instructing the driver to go to the local police station. Joseph looked stricken, but she had courage enough for two. Once there, she paid the fare and ordered him out of the car. With Joseph on her heels, she pushed through the station door and declared that they were looking for a missing person.

'Oh, we got those,' the young sergeant behind the counter replied. 'Coming out of our ears tonight. Not a single one with identification on them. Must be something in the air.'

'We call her Annetta but she calls herself Ann sometimes. Annetta – *Ann* – McVie.'

'Like I said, no one's got ID. What's she wearing?'

Rita looked at Joseph, who was resting on a bench. He shook his head.

'The last time I saw her she was wearing pyjamas. That was earlier today. I mean, yesterday. I wasn't there when she left. I have my own flat.' Then Rita added, 'She takes off her clothes. The doctor says she has dementia.'

'Sundowners,' the sergeant nodded.

'I beg your pardon?'

'Means they have their days and nights confused. They get up when the sun sets and want their breakfast all hours. We get the odd one.' The sergeant looked in his log. 'There's nothing here about birthday suits.'

'White pyjamas printed with rosebuds, then.'

'Excuse me,' the sergeant said, and he disappeared through a door.

Rita sighed. She glanced back at Joseph: huddled, staring at his feet. Like a kicked dog, he was. *Useless*. She looked around the station, at the dirty floor, the cluttered walls, the flyers, the photos, people wanted, people to look out for; smelled the Flash from the corners where the mop splashed. Rita could feel that thousands upon thousands of people had passed through before her, stopped where she stopped, waited and worried and shouted and wept and tried to find an answer. She had been in police stations before, and was nearly collared herself once or twice, but that was more than fifty years ago. Her friends were hauled in and she bailed them out when she could. One girl helped another, back then. She didn't think it was like that now.

When she was on the street, just after the war, soliciting was almost overlooked – until the summer's day when the newspapers, not quite out of news, ran their Soho stories. Smack bang in the middle of the tourist season, slowing a booming trade. Stories about prostitutes and strippers and the nude revues, every kind of temptation for a moral man. Yes, it was true, the politicians said, jumping out of the brothels and into the scrum, each man kicking the next one down until they got to the bottom, where the girls were. The girls were arrested, of course. They pleaded guilty, paid up and went right back to Soho. What else could they do?

Rita hadn't lost her fear of being nicked. The personals were full of women and men selling sex, but she was careful. Who would suspect her? She meant to end her days at home, in her own flat – *not* in the clink getting an earful, begging for mercy.

The sergeant had returned. 'I believe you're in luck. There's a lady downstairs. Not in the cells, mind you. She didn't give us any trouble, only she wouldn't tell us her name. She said she lived in a house but couldn't for the life of her remember where it was.'

*

The Sugar Shop. That's where she wanted to go. Annetta dozed in a chair, a cup of tea going cold beside her. Her torn feet had been bandaged and wore a pair of men's black socks; her hand was dressed in a gauze mitt and she herself was wrapped in a blanket. She could smell the antiseptic and it made her head hurt. All of her hurt, the whole way through – she was old and tired and she wanted comfort. She wanted Nell. Take Wardour Street to Old Compton, follow it to Frith. The Sugar Shop was halfway down on the left. Stairs to climb, then the door – a brown-painted door, battered, needing paint, the bare wood showing through here and there like bone. When she went into the room Nell would be waiting. It was a surprise for her, a party. People crowded round her; then, one by one, they lay down.

Annetta coupled with everyone. That's what she did. She felt herself tingle in the centre of her, where the nerves drew together into a single bead.

The door opened. Annetta blinked. 'Come on,' the man said. 'Your people are here for you.'

'Nell,' she whispered.

'Now you tell us your name. Blood from a stone, I say. Come on, Nell. Time to go home.'

They climbed some stairs. A corridor. A door, two doors, more; she lost count and started over again. A woman and a man – said they would take her. Signing papers. They got into a car with a driver, another man. She looked out of the window. The moon was a dissolving lump of sugar in the early light.

The car stopped, she had no idea where.

She was led.

The state of the house: like a ruined, toothless face; like crumbling statuary, once great. Strung across, a clematis, dead, barbed, hanging by threads. Cigarette butts decorated the step. The front door was frostbitten, blackened in its cracks.

When they went inside, the change in temperature meant she wet herself – the house was boiling, after the chill of the dawn. Rita was always turning up the thermostat. She said it didn't matter about the heating bill, seeing as Arthur Gillies still paid it.

Upstairs, she was washed, towelled dry, dressed in clean pyjamas and put to bed. Annetta had spent more than half her life in bed by then.

'There now, settle down. Mustn't get your knickers in a twist.'

That woman, Annetta thought, not very sure who she was – she thought perhaps her name was Minnie – did nothing but talk, talk, talk all day long.

The woman left the room. While she was out, Annetta went looking for a tiny thing she liked to carry. It charmed her. She was hunting for it in the wardrobe when the woman came back and scolded her to get into bed. The woman said she would tie her down if she had to. She was terrible, she was.

Annetta did as she was told. She lay down and closed her eyes, opened them again. Rita was there. Annetta asked for a kiss. Rita kissed her, smoothed down the covers. Only then could Annetta rest, a hand to her back. She dropped right off to sleep and dreamed of the past.

8

Mr Wye was Annetta's first. He was Arthur Gillies' lawyer, his right-hand man, and his opinion mattered, she was told. Sal said it was the custom that he should meet all the new girls. She called Annetta into the drawing room, where she sat with Mr Wye before a blazing fire. He was tall and thin, with a ghastly grin, dressed all in black except for his shirt: purest white, a shirt just handed to him by his wife. Even in those pea-soup times, when everything was smeared in greasy soot, Mr Wye's collars and cuffs were spotless. Dressed like an undertaker, like he put people in the ground. Annetta wore a long robe of silk and lace and a ribbon in her hair. He looked her over and nodded. She would do. Annetta smiled and took his hand, led him upstairs. He knew where he was going. She was petrified; Sal wanted to see how she handled a man.

Annetta's feet, in new stilettos – she tried not to limp. Her hair, combed of bugs, shone sulphur-yellow in the dim light of the room. The room – hers to keep if Mr Wye liked her – was grand, richly dressed in embroidered satin, with a divan and Chinese cabinets and wallpaper printed with phoenixes.

Once they were alone together, he cleared his throat and asked her, in a quiet voice, to lie down.

Face down, he meant, for he rolled her over. He took her from behind every time, but it wasn't just that; that she didn't mind. It was the other thing: her stockings balled in her mouth and sometimes a pillowslip over her head. He didn't want to see her, hear her, not a peep or murmur. She was to be silent, submissive. Every time he did it the same way. It seemed to go on forever and there was nothing she could do – not if she wanted to maintain her place in the house.

Annetta became a favourite of Mr Wye's. *Rat-a-tat-tat.* Sal would answer the door with a smile and guide him to a chair, but he never wanted to sit long, being there only for one purpose. He wanted to be done with it. Annetta didn't mess about – he'd only hit her. She got into position on the bed. He asked her if she'd washed. She had, more than once that day, for Sal's girls must always be fresh. She was ready for him. She closed her eyes. She went somewhere else.

*

There was never enough money. No one had enough of anything after the war. Even the rich had to cook for themselves, their servants having moved on to labour in the factories, making things that people needed. There was little meat – no chocolate. There was the feeling of having nothing solid on the plate, no weight of coin to make a pocket hang right. They had nothing. Annetta – *Ann*, for she was only Ann then – had missed a childhood of sweets, of rhubarb dipped in sugar and a clementine in her Christmas stocking. Her father shouted, when the table was bare, 'I could kill you!' and she thought he meant it sometimes, to have one less mouth gaping stupidly, to have a little abundance there. She lost two brothers in the war and still the food didn't always stretch to go round.

She had few memories of her dead brothers. They were older, and before the war they hadn't been much at home; they got into trouble, she guessed, from the things people said. The other ones in her family: their *racket*. Raging, always at war. Her mother was a vague, rustling presence. Her father was an ape.

There were places where her bones didn't look to be set right, and a dent under her hair at the back of her head, made when she landed against a doorframe: times when, simply put, the lights went off. She disappeared and no amount of shouting brought her back. She didn't know what they did to her when she wasn't there. She felt things later but she didn't remember. Bruises, cuts, soreness – she just didn't remember.

Where she went, it was dark, but there were watery sounds – waves on a shore – and the sensation was of softness, restfulness, the easing of her body. Pain was at a distance. She could hear voices, but then she could always hear voices. The *so many* of her family, and neighbours close around; the noise of a street crowded with other big families jammed together in a reeking city. Inside herself it was quieter, and the voices spoke kindly, a simple language she could understand.

She hit her head and the world went away.

She flew against the wall and a mirror fell down and broke around her. It was a miracle she wasn't killed, her mother said, but Annetta didn't hear because she wasn't there; she was beyond.

She banged her head against the doorframe and her neck whiplashed.

The dent under her hair.

The bones bent, not set right.

Next thing she knew she was in London. They said there were jobs there and she went looking for a household position. Getting off at Victoria Station, she walked until she found a street lined with grand houses. She feasted her eyes, tasting the air. She looked in windows at tables laid with silver and crystal, laden with hothouse flowers. She just about heard the rustle of full skirts – the New Look that women had started to wear after the war, not that Annetta knew a thing about Christian Dior. After a while she chose a door and knocked to ask if she were needed.

She was at the wrong door, to begin with. She learned to knock at the service door and ask for the housekeeper. She knocked at door after door. She did not look up to the work, one said, meaning Annetta was delicate, meagre. Let me see your hands, said another. Some sneered because she was pretty and they were not; they were coarse, with warts and lined faces and grey hair and they reminded her of horses, the way their teeth stuck out.

She had all the bad luck. She wandered London for days, spent the last of her money and began to starve. She slept behind pillars, inside railings, in parking lots built on bombed-out buildings. Her coat was thin and always wet; the heavens opened on her time and again and she never quite dried out. Her feet rotted in the only pair of shoes she owned, which had belonged to her sister first and were too small.

Annetta finally made her way to Soho. She knew what she would find there – everyone knew it was where the fast set went. First she smelled it: coal, as was everywhere in London, as if the whole city had been fumigated, and then a blast of roasting coffee and vanilla pods. Annetta followed her nose past mysterious herbs for eating and healing, garlic, paprika, mace and fennel, and curry powders in jars – she didn't like *those*. A market smell of earth and potatoes and dung. There were exotic fruits and vegetables to behold, salamis and hams, roasting birds of all sizes that made her mouth water, and cakes she coveted, fresh breads and rolls – long crisp sticks that she longed to snap the end off. She ogled the windows of Camisa's, Lina Stores and Patisserie Valerie. She had no chance of food, being penniless; she must find work first. She picked up a trail of ersatz perfumes, Evening in Paris and Carnation, and, turning onto Old Compton Street, met a throng of women. Annetta went elbow to elbow with any number of fragrant tarts, beautifully turned out at a time when the general population was frayed and worn; having only forty-eight coupons a year, most people wore clothes that hid the grime that poured from the skies. Not the working girls. Many had poodles, coiffed and spoiled creatures, dyed pink and yellow and blue. The bad weather did not trouble them; they grinned and called out to the punters, and their poodles snapped and barked, a real hullaballoo. Girls hung in all the doorways, too, and gathered on the street corners. There were so many! Girls of every kind, all accents – but not good girls, for good girls didn't go to Soho.

Annetta sheltered inside Woolworths, trying to warm up. Her bloodless feet burned as they came to. She didn't notice the woman by the lipsticks, not until she felt strong arms around her. The woman pulled Annetta close, onto her enormous bosom. She smelled of wet wool and body odour and violet perfume. 'You're so cold.'

'Looking for work all day,' Annetta muttered. It was nice, being held, but she didn't know the woman from Adam.

'They're hiring here. If you worked here, then I'd know where to find you.' The woman released her.

'They're hiring?'

'I'm Nell, by the way.'

'I'm Ann.'

Nell offered her a lipstick. 'You're blue in the lips. And your hands – rub them together. Tuck yourself in. You need a scarf to hide that collar. That's better. Now off you go,' she said.

Annetta soon returned. 'I start Monday.'

'What did I tell you? What did I say? This calls for a celebration,' Nell grinned. 'I know – we'll stop off at Lyons.'

Annetta had never been but naturally had heard of the place. Everyone knew Lyons' teashops, the most famous in the world. Nell led Ann from floor to floor, pointing out the marvels of the decor, the marble columns and chandeliers and the thick carpet that muted the clatter of cups and saucers. The Nippy uniform was everywhere, charging forth through swinging doors, dashing among the many tables. Nell seemed to know all the girls by name and waved hello or blew a kiss or goosed them as they passed at speed. Finally they sat down in the Grill & Cheese, where they took a long time to eat and drink their tea.

Nell was full of advice. She mustn't let the city beat her down, Nell said. There was plenty of work – Annetta just had to look in the right places. Nell had been there ten years already, a country girl herself, just the hearty rustic sort London liked to devour. But London wouldn't get her, Nell vowed, and she had mothered a good many others as well. Everywhere she looked she saw lost souls kicking about. She only wanted to help them. 'You're a lovely thing, too,' Nell said, stroking Annetta's hand. 'A real good baby, I can tell.'

After Lyons, Nell bought her the clothes she needed – new shoes and fur-lined gloves, a red blouse – and promised a better coat from a department store. She pointed out the bombsites in St Martin's Lane where children played cowboys and Indians, the Maltese gangsters, the ponces and pimps, the evangelical rescuers, the tourists with money to spend, the pill dealers, the Italian waiters who looked at girls with their hearts in their eyes. Then Nell took Annetta to her room above the Sugar Shop, homely as it was, the bed covered in a pretty eiderdown and, next to it, an electric fire – there was even a chintz armchair in one corner. Annetta bathed in the tin bath and Nell put her to bed. Under cover of night: striving fingers, kisses, the bedclothes a mess.

Annetta's shifts at Woolworths were spent in a daze of wonder and fatigue, for Nell talked constantly, all hours, as well as doing the other things. This is love, she told herself, feeling exhilarated, electric; feeling it to be true, all the nonsense. Love made her sick to her stomach, sleepless even when she might have rested, with Nell finally passed out beside her in bed, when she gazed at her lover, marvelling at every mutter and twitch. Love was real, and yet she could hardly believe Nell existed; a woman to whom she was so perfectly matched, who understood Annetta without her having to explain herself.

A week or two passed like that before Nell asked her a favour. She didn't like to ask, but she was in a pickle. A friend had let her down—

She hated to ask, Nell said.

When it was over and the gentleman had crept off, leaving ten pounds on the pillow, they fell into each other's arms.

'Were you afraid?' Nell asked.

'Not with you there,' Annetta replied.

'Was it very bad for you?'

Annetta shook her head. They both knew she would do it again, that she had enjoyed herself enough. It wasn't what she felt with Nell, but it had its own excitement. Nell was pleased. She had thought Annetta would like it. She said that Annetta must give herself another name if she were going to pick up the life. When Annetta asked why, she replied, 'You think my name is Nell?'

Annetta had never questioned it. Nothing else would suit her. 'What's your name, then?'

'I'm not telling. I never tell. Whatever it is, I won't have it on my gravestone.'

'Tell me,' Annetta begged.

'It's not my name. It's not who I am.'

'Who are you?' Annetta wondered, and she said it so sweetly, with pure wonder, that Nell laughed.

'You want a sweet name. Something sweet as sugar, like you. Something like . . . Fanny. That's you. Sweetness through and through.'

'It's dirty,' Annetta said. Nell laughed again. She was always laughing at Annetta. Then Nell rolled down her stockings – the last bits of clothing she still wore.

In that cosy room above the Sugar Shop, music coming up from downstairs, Annetta felt herself *be*. The person she was with Nell: that's who she really was. The past was erased – she had done it, wiped it clean. She was someone else entirely from the girl she had been with her family. It was the strangest thing.

'Oh darling, my Annetta,' Nell sighed.

*

After that, if there was a man who wanted a young girl or more than one girl, Nell fetched Annetta to the room above the Sugar Shop. Annetta couldn't deny the money she made with Nell was good, for the men were rich, but she kept her job at Woolworths all the same. Between the two she could afford to eat at Lyons whenever she wanted.

It turned out that most of Soho did what she did, even the ones who said they didn't; they could be bought for enough money at the end of the month when their bills were due. Then there were the casuals who dropped in and out of the trade – housewives, single mothers, war widows. There seemed to be so many working girls, and always very busy, no matter the time of day.

Sometimes Nell was flushed with drink, when she called Annetta her filly and knocked her around the room. When Annetta opened her eyes, having gone elsewhere, deep in the cool dark that whispered, Nell was always distraught. Annetta forgave her, and gifts were made in the aftermath: bottles of scent, flowers, chocolates, although making up was sweet enough for Annetta.

Woolworths gave her the sack when she skipped off with Nell halfway through a shift to meet a punter. She moved on to a stationer's, then a launderette, but Nell always came along with a better offer. Annetta took a job in a cafe, only to set down the coffee pot she had been about to pour when Nell turned up and whispered in her ear. She sold buttonholes, she pamphleted, but always she was waiting for Nell to appear. The hours they were apart were to be endured; Annetta only lived when Nell was around, or so she felt. She thought of nothing but Nell. She was possessed – she was madly in love. Annetta had known for some time that she was unnatural, but Nell confirmed it. Nell was the same; she was with those men for the money, nothing more.

'My mother took me to a doctor, looking for a cure. He told her to put me in a convent. I told them I'd have a good time in there,' Nell laughed. 'That's when they kicked me out. What about you?'

'What?'

'What were you kicked out for?'

'Who says I was kicked out? I just left.'

'Why?'

'I don't remember.'

'You don't remember,' Nell said. 'That's impossible. That's just covering your tracks.'

There was the one thing, when she was nine. She couldn't remember, oh, maybe a bit – the familiar grin from certain men, and one of them once said almost the exact words her uncle had: 'You must have been a sexy little girl.' When Annetta looked at their shoes and saw broken knotted laces and worn rubber soles scooped out in half-moons at the back, her breath cut short – but how often did she see that? Rich men paid a price for her that the working class couldn't afford. The rich wore handmade shoes, sleek as skinned cats.

Her uncle, with an unwashed smell on him that crossed a room, stole from her mother even though there was nothing to steal. Annetta remembered that. He stole money from his sister's purse and stole the baking from her larder, pinching a pie crust until the top collapsed, twirling the custard with a filthy finger, strip-mining the jolliest bits of a fruit loaf. Fat when times were lean. Then he went for her daughters. He was married, but no one knew where his wife was. Under the rose bushes, some said.

He wouldn't leave Annetta alone. She tried to tell, but he just said that she'd always been a tart. He would know, Annetta said.

Nell had it as well, from a brother. She shrugged. 'It wasn't much.'

'I just don't remember,' Annetta said, and she wasn't lying. 'I don't know why. I can't seem to keep things in my head. Mum said it was because I didn't pay attention. She thought I was simple, a bit.'

'Was it bad?'

Annetta nodded. It seemed a long time ago, another life. She had endured her uncle, and the general violence of her childhood: the razor strap, the hairbrush, a wooden kitchen spoon, the back of a hand – but everyone had the razor strap, the hairbrush, a wooden kitchen spoon, the back of a hand, every blooming child she knew, and some, like her, had worse.

'There's a lot I wish I could forget. Some old boy gobbed in my tea when I was in Bar Italia the other day. Said he wouldn't pay a farthing for a trollop like me.'

'What did you do?'

'I put on my brightest smile and picked up my cup like to drink from it, didn't I? I've had worse than that in my mouth,' Nell laughed. No one laughed like Nell.

*

How Annetta floated through those weeks, full of secret thoughts of Nell's long breasts curled up in a lacy brassiere, the way her hips mushroomed, a line of cherry-coloured moles snaking down one leg. Nell's eyes: dark as flint, thickly lashed, eyes that streamed when she laughed.

Annetta took a job answering phones. She told Nell to ring her anytime. It was perfect. 'Ring and I'll come to you,' she said.

'I'll call you every hour,' Nell promised. 'Just to hear your voice.'

She called once in the morning to laugh at the novelty of it and then she didn't call again. All day Annetta waited, choking on 'hello' as the hours passed and Nell still didn't ring. At the end of her shift, she went straight to Nell's room above the Sugar Shop. The door stood open. Only the bed remained, and it looked to be broken.

Annetta sat down on the floor and felt her heart would break. It wasn't done yet – it couldn't be done, for they had only just started. They had dreamed a whole life together, the music coming up from downstairs while they lay in bed and talked and laughed and made love: the promises Nell made when it got late. All night Annetta waited in that room but Nell did not return. In the morning, having not slept, she went down to the street to look. She asked everyone she met and sought out Nell's friends but no one knew where she was. Some said it was drink, a bender she was on. Some said it was another woman, an old love from whom Nell could never escape. Others said she had met a man who swept her off her feet, who had enough money to take care of everything. No one said she was dead, but Annetta feared the worst. It had happened before: girls in the river and the canals, girls in pieces by the tracks. Nobody cared when girls were found like that, except the other girls.

Annetta walked down to the Embankment and picked through the drunks lumped together in rags; she pulled at mute bodies, rolled them over to get a look at the face. She retched sometimes. 'Nell? Nell?' They spat at her, or tried to lift her skirt. Some lay utterly still as if waiting to die, eyes glazed: lights out.

She took a job wearing a sandwich board with an arrow pointing *THIS WAY FOR A BARGAIN*. Every so often she called out, loud and clear, 'Nell!'

No Nell.

One day she bumped into an old friend of Nell's, a regular called John. He tapped the sandwich board. 'What have you got on under there?'

'Wouldn't you like to know?'

'What do you say we walk round the corner? I know a hotel – nice rooms, clean sheets.'

Annetta hesitated. Soho hummed around her. The sandwich board hid her shabby clothes, full of holes. Her shoes were lined with cardboard. She needed the money. No one would notice if she went off with John, and they would be quick enough, if she knew the man.

He grew impatient. 'Where's your friend? Where's Nell? She wouldn't make me wait like this.'

She told him that Nell was in the south of France with her grandmother. Nell was looking after her sick auntie up north. Nell was visiting her brother in Ireland, where he worked in the police squad. It didn't matter what she said: Nell was gone. When he looked surprised, she said, 'You think we don't have people.' For the married men who sought the likes of Annetta and Nell, they were the cure for the wife, the queen who reigned at home, prematurely aged, dried out, distracted by children and their crying needs, their streaming noses and bedtime drinks and spills and bumps that made them weep as if their hearts were breaking: their absolute neediness. Men like John, they just wanted a bit of fun. It was nothing. It was relief, that's all; it didn't matter who the woman was.

'I always liked you best. You were the sweetest of Nell's girls. A real innocent.' He tapped the sandwich board again. 'Let's get you into something more comfortable.'

Others followed – *tap, tap* on the sandwich board and off they went. Soho was free and easy then. The busy streets afforded their own privacy, having been built for pleasure, not commerce: down an alley, even a doorway would do. Or, if the punter had money, they found themselves a room, for many hotels rented by the hour.

The kind of life she led did not mean that she wasn't good. She was honest about what she did – at least she was that. What did honest mean? What did they mean when they said she wasn't an honest woman? She understood perfectly what she did, and what she didn't: she didn't steal or cheat. She worked. She had always worked; she came from a working-class family, the ethic, the exhortation to *work* passed down like a good set of china.

Annetta had started outside the home when she was eleven, picking strawberries, stooped over a field of fruit, arms aching, fingers torn and stinging, eyes scalded by the sun. Then she washed dishes. Scrubbed bogs. Plucked chickens. Made sausage, grappling with the squeaky intestine. Nothing bothered her. She caught spiders in her hands and threw them out of the windows of her frightened mistresses.

A girl could still walk single in Soho in those days. Annetta's back ached from working in high heels until three or four in the morning; her feet were on fire, burning with pain, but at least it wasn't like huddling over a sloppy floor with a cold rag cramping her hand. That's what she told herself. She walked slowly between restaurants and bars – there were so many girls doing just the same. She dressed up in colourful dresses and stuck a rhinestone pin in her hair, hoping to stand out, but the truth was all working girls dressed like film stars.

Annetta had her beat on Romilly Street, bought from a French girl who was going home, a real Fifi with a poodle in her arms. Annetta worked the street but she might ride in a car if she got the right feeling, just to have the change of scenery. She loved getting out into the countryside, especially late at night when the sky was so very black and she had no sense of where the road was going.

She was eighteen but she looked like a baby doll. No matter how rich or poor, a man paid the same: £5 a go, and it seemed a fair amount for what was sometimes the work of minutes. She could make £100 a night on the ten-minute rule if she wanted to. She'd heard about the pampered high-class girls who were making hundreds by the hour, who had their own flats in Mayfair and all the clothes and jewellery they could wish for. She heard about girls who kept their careers brief, about a year, and then went on to marry stock-brokers.

In winter Annetta's legs went blue, then swelled to a beefy red when she thawed indoors. The older walkers had lumps of fat buttressing their calves and veins something terrible and there were mornings they could hardly get their shoes on, they said. They'd be off to the East End soon, was the joke.

Walk between the raindrops. Close your eyes. Hold your breath. It would soon be over. Annetta learned not to be there when they touched her but sometimes she felt a stranger's hands gripping her too hard, or saw, as if from outside herself, a man suckling her breast and she wondered how she could ever let them do that.

One afternoon, Annetta found herself in front of the Sugar Shop. Her feet often took her there but usually she hurried past, once she'd made certain that Nell still hadn't returned. That day, she stopped. She climbed the stairs. The door swung open as if Nell were behind it, already half undressed. The soaped windows. The bed in two. The walls papered in streaks and layers and the bare bulb overhead, fiercely bright. Her breath caught. 'Oh God,' she said, remembering Nell's lips, the yellow skin around her eyes, puckered and thin, and her gypsy hair in a plait down her back, almost to her waist. Her handsomeness, her height and breadth, her deep solidity and the dimpled, casually gathered flesh. Annetta fell to her knees and wept.

The next day she moved in. She fixed the bed and bought the things she needed. She had cards printed for the phone boxes: *Large Chest for Sale*. She hired a maid, a pockmarked girl from Lancaster, to change the linen and rinse the bath and brew the tea. Here come the millionaires, the maid would say, ducking out of the way when they heard a knock at the door. One of them, Philip, who built hotels, kept calling her Hannah but Annetta didn't mind. She would be who they wanted.

*

Sylvain was not rich, but his shirts were silk – they showed his ribs. His nose was crooked, a broken-looking thing, his bottom lip seamed and swollen, chewed on, sometimes white in its cracks with the medicated balm he used. He was a pusher, although Annetta at least had the sense not to touch his tablets and powders. He peddled on the streets – he was everywhere she looked, around every Soho corner she turned. If he caught her eye he smiled, a real, genuine smile. When he finally spoke to her, he made her laugh. What a relief to laugh! She collapsed with laughter and she couldn't seem to stop. He loved to make her laugh. Just to be with him, laughing, was nice, without the rest of it, but that happened, too. People said he was a ponce but Annetta was already in love with him. He soon moved into her room above the Sugar Shop. He was homeless, otherwise, living in the bars and clubs, friends with every doorman in town. He had a way with people, something to do with his imprisonment during the war. It was hell, he told her, but he didn't starve, and he was kept in cigarettes as well.

She waited with a towel for his hair when it rained, cushions to pad his bones, the teapot in one hand and hot buttered toast in the other. When he undressed he threw away his socks, and he never bothered with underwear. In the bath he groaned with pleasure, pinking up like a cooked prawn. He had to scrub hard to remove the city from his skin; he dipped his hands in bleach to whiten them. In Annetta's cheap room above the Sugar Shop, with the music coming up from downstairs, he luxuriated before the three-bar fire like a deerhound on the hearth, worn out with flushing the crowd to turn out a buyer. He dozed and started, jumping to – he never slept more than an hour at a time. He called Annetta his dolly, his baby love. Sylvain had no ejaculatory control and he had a way of looking at her, slightly dazed, that made her think he loved her.

He wanted her hair a different way. He wanted her to wear certain things, black-market finery, mostly indecent, and red nails, red lips. He didn't want her to go with the Americans and brought her instead the soldiers who had developed their habits during the war and who complained to him that the government dried up their supply. 'This is Annetta,' Sylvain would say and join their hands together.

'What do I need her for? I got a wife at home,' some replied, but it was the married ones who always paid up first.

If there were more than one they took it in turns, waiting outside in the corridor, Sylvain in last of all.

'How much did you take?'

'I don't know,' she shrugged, the money already stuffed in a cushion. 'Will I see you later?'

He wiped the sweat from her face. 'Wash yourself,' he said. 'You smell like a cat's arse.'

With Sylvain around, her regulars disappeared, but there were always new customers. She saw knives, she got hit and scratched and bitten. Sometimes she went deep inside herself, but she always returned to find a man on top of her, bearing down. When she complained that it was too many men, Sylvain told her to shut it. Those men were war heroes, he said.

The world had changed. The world had seen things – people could not believe what had happened. Believe it, they were told. The men who came back from the war were damaged, missing parts, blinded, ruined, scarred with burns. They suffered, how they suffered. Their wives, they said, weren't the same. The children didn't remember them, or remembered a different man. They had children they didn't think were theirs. Their children were frightened of them: their injuries, field-stitched, still wept and soaked the bandages, or they sat in stony silence, preoccupied with battle scenes they could not forget. There was not enough work, no homes to buy even if they could have afforded them. Annetta took their five pounds and closed her eyes and prayed they wouldn't hurt her.

Listen to what they want, Sylvain said. No talking, just

listening. Give them what they want. She listened. Their stories made her stomach turn. More than one man had cried in her bed – they couldn't get it up, they said. The war had taken that from them. The war rubbed her all over. She picked up nits, scabies, shingles, the stuff of the trenches, and there was something wrong with her feet. She couldn't stand for long, not without them aching so much she thought she might faint with the pain. It was a reason not to go streetwalking, to stay in her room above the Sugar Shop and let Sylvain handle her trade.

He brought her men, more men, coming and going, day and night, yet somehow she was always plumping that cushion of hers and feeling air between the feathers where the notes should have been. He never asked for a cut like most ponces did, and if he was taking one anyway, she didn't know. He shook tablets at her but she said no. She slept when she could. Her eyelids scratched, clicking open. Sometimes she craved the beyondness a blow to the head brought.

The ordeal of a rotten mouth, a tongue that was just a tongue, a pushing thing, another pushing thing trying to find a way in, and filthy hands that wanted to have a go as well, and the crude tattoos, the wounds, the festering wounds, baroque of palette, rich with pain: the stink of men, soldiers and sailors and general vagrants, who thought nothing of screwing when they hadn't had a wash for a week.

She should have stayed away from Sylvain. He had the smell and feel of medicine to him, his fingertips lightly dusted as if with talc – not like the hands of the men she had known growing up, who worked in factories and on farms, men who made things, their hands calloused, lightly abrasive, stained with tobacco, the nails broken, ingrained. Hands that would catch on a whore's chemise.

Sylvain gave her a fur piece that smelled of another woman. A blouse of gold satin that was missing buttons. Ferragamo shoes with scuffed soles that didn't fit but he insisted she wear anyway. The things came to her in a blur. She just couldn't wake up.

One night he brought six noisy, addled punters to her room. Annetta was wearing a new dress, bright red. 'That your bridal gown?' Sylvain said, making everyone laugh. He didn't love her. She would never be the one he loved. She began to cry, her eyes filling and her shoulders going like she had the hiccups, but still she had to take those men, two of them amputees. Sylvain came last, cursing her under his breath, saying the bed stank of rotten flesh. He wanted some money – he grabbed it off her. She locked the door behind him and wept until she slept. She slept like she was dead.

Next thing she knew he was back with more men, at least three or four, and they threatened to kick down the door. Annetta quaked but she didn't get out of bed. She couldn't. Her body had given up. All night long there were men up and down the stairs, banging and shouting, calling her a slapper, a treacherous bitch. She dared not move, dared hardly breathe lest they hear.

The rest of that long night she listened – she strained her ears to hear. Hurrying footsteps, a smutty song, police sirens, and finally, come dawn, the scrape of a handcart, rowdy vendors warming up their voices with coffee and whisky. She was still there and Sylvain was gone.

She let herself doze and then someone was at the door – a different knock, friendly, joking. Shave and a haircut, six bits. A woman's voice said, 'Nell? Are you there, Nell? It's me.' She knocked again. 'Nell?'

'There's no Nell here,' Annetta said.

'Oh, come on, Nell. It's me. Rita. From the Cul de Sac.'

'Who?' Annetta said.

'Rita. They said you got married. They said you were dead. Someone said you turned up on a building site with a brick in your head. How about that? I knew you couldn't be dead, Nell. Not you.'

'What do you want?'

'Only to say hello. I was on my way to Lyons.'

'Anyone with you?'

'Just me.'

'How do I know?'

'Open the door, Nell. I've had enough of this now.'

Annetta opened the door. The girl who stood there looked about her own age, dark eyes and hair and features so angular they seemed to have been drawn with one strong line. Rita, she had said her name was. 'I'm not Nell, as you can see, but for God's sake come in.'

'Have you got trouble?'

'What do you know?' Annetta said. 'Who are you? I never seen you before in my life.'

'I'm a friend of Nell's.'

'What kind of friend?'

'Just a friend,' Rita laughed. 'But I haven't seen her around.'

'I don't know where she is.'

'Has she been gone long?'

Annetta didn't answer.

'Did she say where she was going?'

'She's not here. There was nothing here. Just the bed, and that was in pieces, but I managed to mend it well enough.'

'One of life's necessities,' Rita said, patting it. 'I know this old rocking horse, don't I?'

Annetta looked at her: striking, slim, with a noble bust, but there was a hardness about her, skin like marble, luminous, well moulded and cold. 'I suppose you do.'

'I'm not like that. I only meant—'

'You better go now.'

'I haven't got anywhere to go, have I? Nell's seen to that.'

'I don't know.'

'Don't know what?' Rita said.

'About Nell.' Annetta felt the tears start, but there was nothing she could do to stop them. It was talking about Nell that did it; she would never get over her.

'It wasn't like that between me and Nell.'

'Like what?'

'I don't love her, if that's what you're asking.'

'I'm so lonely without her!' Annetta wailed.

Rita said, 'I could stay. Just for a cup of tea, if you're having one. I could do with a cup of tea myself – I was on my way to Lyons when I stopped.'

For days after, Annetta shook and was sick – that was the tablets going out of her, Rita said. 'But I didn't. I never touched the stuff. I swear I never did,' Annetta protested.

'He must have found a way. They think they're magicians.' Rita wiped Annetta's face with a cool flannel. 'Just rest now.'

9

Arthur had been one of a majestic presence of soldiers in Chiusi. They smiled – how the soldiers smiled when the war went their way. They shook hands with the men and winked at the women and teased the children, offering them broken chocolate bars. They spoke no Italian and the Italians spoke no English but everything was understood between them: these men were heroes. Arthur smiled especially at Flavia, who sat in the jagged, foreshortened shade of a building that had until recently been whole. With their eyes only they talked all afternoon, looking, smiling, laughing, fawning. Finally he stepped over to her and they made an assignation, writing with a stick in the dust of the road. That evening, hours early, she went to wait in the shadows of the bombed-out trattoria he had named, where they were sure to be hidden from view.

The dusk settled around her while she waited; cats crept past her knees, searching for food among the ruins. She could hardly stand it. She put her head in her arms: he was late. He was not coming. He had made a promise he did not intend to keep. She was always afraid of the dark, but that night the dark hid her shame. She was humiliated. She wanted him – she wanted him more for not wanting her. She waited. He never came. She was stiff in the morning, helping her mother with the housework. When she finally saw him later in the day, he sought her eyes, took her arm, tried to explain the duties of a soldier. He followed her into her mother's kitchen and inhaled the scent of the thin vegetable stock that would become soup for the family. He rubbed his stomach. He pointed to her eyes and smiled and said something. Shit-brown eyes, he was saying – she didn't know what he was saying. Already she could sense his will: that she would believe what he told her.

It was not that her parents forbade the marriage; it was the way Arthur wanted to go about things: no hanging around for her extended family to gather themselves, every last cousin to arrive and the lot of them to file past the table where the happy couple sat with their glasses of Frangelico and *millefoglie*. It would take months that way. Better to run off and be done with it. So she left with Arthur one night while her family was sleeping, with just a change of clothes and a comb and toothbrush to see her through the long journey. She met him at the bombed-out trattoria and they caught a ride on an army truck that was shipping out. They took buses and trains and finally a boat that chugged across the English Channel, dodging the detritus of vessels that had been shot down or sunk in the war. When they landed in England, Arthur kissed the ground, much to the delight of onlookers, while she hung shyly at his side and kept her mouth shut. He had told her they didn't like Italians in England – people thought they were all fascists. She gathered his meaning from what little she understood of what he said: Italian Fascismo, he repeated, and she nodded.

She had been reconciled with her family later but she had not seen them again. Her parents were already old when she left – she was the youngest of nine children – and they died before her first year in England was out. She was desolate when those letters arrived, first one and then the other, a few months later. She replaced the letters in their envelopes, as if that would do the trick, and put them away in a drawer. For all she knew, having not looked at them since, the smell of home was still on the pages.

Arthur did not understand her grief, and there was still the language barrier between them. He held her for a bit and then he wanted his supper. They were dead and buried, he said. Times were different. We're up against it – that's what people thought. Make do and mend. Carry on. They were down at heel, rationed. Later, from a brother with a camera, came a photograph of the grave her parents shared, along with a snip of the myrtle that had been planted there. Flavia kept both in a polished silver frame by her bed, next to a photo of Arthur in his army uniform, and she bade them all goodnight before she went to sleep at the end of a long day of housekeeping.

Of his own parents, Arthur said little. No point in raking over that old muck. Is that what he said? Her English was very poor and sometimes he spoke so fast, so gruff. Did he have brothers and sisters? Yes, but he didn't get on with them. His father had been a true Victorian. Arthur didn't remember him touching or seeming to care at all about his children. Children, for a man like his father, were there to work: daughters to help their mother with the house, sons to learn a trade. Arthur wanted more than that. He wanted to go up in the world. He liked to think of himself as above class. He was, by definition, working class, but it was the company he kept that he felt would come to define him: the kind of men he'd known during the war, when he'd found himself tossed together with every kind of Englishman.

After they married, Arthur and Flavia settled in Kettering where Arthur, who had been a pipe fitter before the war, took a job as a machinist in a boot factory. They found a bedsit and Flavia kept it clean and provided delicious meals with cheap bits of meat: the tongue, the tail, the feet. Everything in one room, that's how they lived. She cooked on a hotplate. Their milk was on the window ledge. Every penny must go to the future, Arthur said.

One day he went to London to meet up with a few of his army brothers. He had a new suit to wear – he said it would not do for them to see him dressed as a pauper. 'All we ever talked about was what we would get up to after it was all over. They want to see the big man, I'll give them the big man.' He spent a long time getting ready, fastidious with his hair, which had begun to recede despite the tonics and oils he used faithfully – an extravagance he felt he was owed for his hard work in the boot factory.

She must not wait up, he said. What they wanted to do was drink and talk late into the night and he would take the milk train home. But Flavia waited. She had no choice in the matter: she was afraid of the dark. She had never told him; she had pretended otherwise, and about other things, too, she had pretended she didn't mind, like him going to the pub after work without sending word home to her, when she had cooked all day to make him something he liked. And when he came in late and followed her around, lifting her dress, she always let him have his way.

But that night, every time she put her head down on the pillow she thought she heard footsteps on the stairs, an eyeball to the keyhole roaming the cool dark: an intruder, come to get her. When Arthur finally appeared at dawn, she was frantic, in tears. He didn't seem to notice but scooped her into his arms and whirled her around until she laughed. Then they went to bed. They slept the day away. She had never done that before, stayed in bed all of a day and through the night. When Marie came to be.

*

Marie, not Maria, as Flavia had wished, but the flatter, more English Marie. Arthur liked the name. She was a ten-pounder, one of those: gigantic, ruddy from the moment they squealed, great rolls of fat in their arms and legs, having been reared inside on Sunday roasts and sticky toffee pudding, stuffed like ducks for foie gras; who came out hungry for lamb and potatoes, carbonara, *melanzane alla parmigiana*, fillet steak, pork chops – but learned to content themselves with mother's milk and drained their mothers dry.

When Marie was born, Flavia didn't know where Arthur was. She hadn't seen him since he dropped her at the hospital that morning; he found her a porter and fled. Her pains were bearable at first; then, in the evening, the pattern tightened – drew into a wailing prayer that she would die, and at that moment the baby crowned. Arthur briefly appeared to learn he had a daughter and to touch her small head. He kissed Flavia and told her she had done very well and he would see her in a few days, when her confinement was over. He reminded her that he didn't like hospitals or doctors; they made him sick – he, who was the picture of stout good health.

Flavia and the baby, Marie, eventually went home and began their long life together. By then Arthur lived away during the week, having gone into business in London with an army friend, only returning home at weekends. Things had happened quickly for him: by the time Marie was born he had left the boot factory, earning enough in six months to buy them a semi-terraced house, pebble-dashed, north-facing, with a magnolia tree out front. Fully furnished. London was no place to raise a family, in his opinion; better to settle in Kettering, where there was plenty of affordable housing, not blown to bits as it was in the capital. Arthur didn't know then that he would work in London all his life.

All week Flavia waited for him. She tended to Marie ceaselessly – a colicky baby, whose crying and coughing gave Flavia much worry. By the time Arthur arrived home every Friday night, shortly after nine o'clock, she was on her knees. Then, blessed relief, just to have him there.

She poured him a drink in the fine glass bought just for that purpose – whisky, three fingers – eased his shoes from his feet and helped him with his slippers. She retrieved his supper from the oven, steaming under foil, and watched his face while he ate. She sat up late with him, until he was ready for bed, then double-checked the locks and turned out the lights: Arthur home again, safe, her family under one roof, asleep. Flavia said a prayer of thanks.

Saturday morning she cooked him breakfast while he put the baby on his knee and bounced her until she cried. After breakfast, Flavia showed him her weekly housekeeping and he examined the bills and receipts. He admired her way with money: how well they ate on so little. It did not occur to her to ask him for more than he gave. She made a big lunch, eaten in silence, before he settled into his chair with the newspapers. At five o'clock sharp she handed him a glass of whisky and fed Marie her tea while 'Tampico' played on the gramophone. He wanted peace and quiet when he didn't want 'Tampico'.

After Marie had eaten her tea, Flavia bathed her and chose a pretty nightdress, all lace, then showed her off to Arthur: a sallow comma who didn't suit pink. Later, Marie howled while they ate.

'Leave her,' Arthur barked at Flavia. 'You spoil her.'

But she couldn't, she just couldn't leave Marie to cry it out. 'Her colic,' she pleaded with him.

Arthur did not understand. He wanted things the way he wanted them. Once Marie was settled, Flavia sat with him while he drank another whisky. They listened to the Third Programme on the wireless or they listened to 'Tampico', whichever he preferred. Flavia tried to stay awake – how she willed herself and shook her head and rubbed her eyes – but more than once she woke alone in the dark sitting room, Arthur having taken himself off to bed and left her there in a chair: cold, uncovered.

On Sunday there was another meal to prepare and Flavia rose early, taking Marie downstairs with her. Later, Arthur would appear, having had a bath, and smile at them both and drink a cup of tea and eat his eggs and toast while he read the papers, and Flavia would think to herself that all was well in the world.

After lunch, if the sun shone, they sat out in the garden on a rug with one of Flavia's cakes cut into generous slices, the baby asleep in her pram. Arthur snored, his head in Flavia's lap. She stroked his cheek, ran a finger over the smudges of his eyebrows and sighed with contentment.

Sometimes he wanted to watch the cricket in the park and she might go along provided she kept the baby quiet. She watched, proud at her husband's side. The game was incomprehensible to her: young men windmilling their arms and finally throwing a ball, all of them aglow in whites. When Arthur's eyes followed other women, she flushed, made a fuss over something – a kamikaze wasp, stinger erect, headed in their direction, or the wind that struck up like a band, the sun in the baby's eyes – just to draw his attention again.

Love *me*, she begged silently.

Then it was time to think about Arthur going back to London. By mid afternoon on Sunday he was ready to go. She felt his readiness: it was palpable. He could hardly sit still. The baby was of no interest. He wanted to get dressed – where was his suit? His shoes? Everything was ready upstairs in the wardrobe. She heard him brush his teeth and then he was a long time before the mirror, his feet creaking that particular floorboard. Flavia tried not to cry. Sometimes he wanted her to clip his nails. Sometimes he called downstairs for her to play 'Tampico'.

She made him sandwiches for the train from whatever roast they'd had. A hard-boiled egg. A slice of cake. An apple, cored. Flask of tea.

He pecked her on the cheek the same way he stamped the baby on the head: hard, dry lips, mouth sealed, nothing thrilling about it. Then he was off.

*

The doorbell rang. Marie, with a bowl of porridge before her on the tray of her high chair, startled and let out a siren wail at the sound of the bell.

Flavia, who was tired, always alone with a baby who would not sleep; Flavia, all nerves, jumpy like the skin had been flayed from her; Flavia could not think who was at the door. The gas man? The fishmonger? It wasn't Thursday.

Was it? When she was so tired, it was hard to think. It wasn't Friday – she knew what Fridays felt like. Was it June already? The birds sang so early, the sun set so late, or so it seemed to Flavia, who only wanted to sleep.

Flavia was a prisoner, a hostage. She adored her keeper and dreaded her just the same: a knot in the pit of her stomach. Marie never slept, never smiled, often screamed as if she had a pain. Flavia knew she must go to her, put Marie over her shoulder and walk her again, the jigging walk that quieted her; a joyless baby always wanting to be held, always needing something, wet, tired, hungry, but only taking a little bit. 'Drink,' Flavia urged her daughter, giving her a bottle. 'Please,' she begged, but Marie would only take a fraction of what her mother thought she needed. Flavia watched the kitchen clock all day. She tried to get the housework done but found she couldn't; Marie needed picking up and soothing, her nappy changed, the whole of her stripped of soiled garments and dressed all over again. There seemed always to be some kind of leak from Marie. Sometimes Flavia was glad that Arthur was not there to see the state of the house and his wife so rumpled, her housedress spotted and stained where she wiped her hands all day, her black coils of hair sprouting grey.

Oh, but if he were there just to take the baby off in her pram for an hour, even half an hour, then Flavia could have a bath, the long, hot soak she craved—

Marie didn't seem to like him much. If ever he held her, she wailed. Perched on his knee, she leaned away from him, eyes wide. 'She wants you,' he called to Flavia in the kitchen.

He was not one for making nice with babies; he did not pat or talk in a silly voice or blow kisses. He wouldn't change her nappy. When Marie cried during the night, Flavia always raced to her cot lest Arthur wake. He was very particular about his sleep.

The doorbell. Flavia answered: a telegram. She'd never had one before. She had to get a neighbour to read the message aloud to her. Upon hearing it, Flavia burst into tears. The neighbour said, did she feel well? Did she feel quite right? Was she sure? Flavia nodded and was shown to the door with a biscuit for Marie. Back in her own home, she cried more – Marie pointed at her and laughed, so funny, Flavia's face like that.

The telegram said that Arthur wouldn't arrive until the following weekend. Business kept him in London.

Flavia, unclean as a madwoman, hair like a hedgerow because she hadn't the time to sit with a hairbrush and make it shine; Flavia, who drank cold tea and ate slices of buttered bread because there was no chance to cook something; Flavia, forever rinsing nappies, soaking nappies, washing nappies by hand, wringing them, nappies on a clothes line strung across the kitchen, so many nappies – Flavia suffered.

He wouldn't be home until next weekend.

A hundred years from then.

*

She counted the days and then the hours. Friday was the longest day; she had everything to do. She cleaned the house from top to bottom and cooked a good meal; all the while Marie howled to be picked up. She would just have to wait, Flavia told her. There were candles and flowers and she had the fire going red-hot in the sitting room. She bathed and dressed carefully after Marie was in bed – she put Marie down early, with finger curls in her hair in case Arthur wanted to see her. Flavia couldn't recall that he ever did. A sleeping baby should sleep, he said. Once or twice, when he'd had an extra drink, she knew that he looked in on her, but he didn't wish for her to wake.

He would be home soon. Flavia smoothed the new dress. It was wine-coloured wool crepe with a sweetheart neckline. Sweetheart necklines had been all the rage when she was a girl, and she had been wearing a dress with a sweetheart neckline when she met Arthur – pink batiste, a dress her Aunt Cecelia made for her. She wore it again the night she ran off with him. On the train, three days into their long journey to England, when she really needed a wash, he had led her to a narrow vestibule where the luggage was piled high. He buried his face in her cleavage and lifted her skirt, sticking his hand up there. She had clung to him as the train bumped and swung – she felt as though her knees would give way. His hand, *there*.

Flavia thought she looked nice. The house shone around her. There was nothing to do but wait.

She thought that maybe tonight they would be together like they used to, Arthur having reached for her in the dark. He still did sometimes. She was always very quiet, not wanting to wake Marie and hear her fuss and feel that she must go to her. Arthur didn't like that. Usually by the time she got back to bed he'd sorted himself out and fallen asleep.

That's how it went. The slights, the hurts, the black marks: not tallied up but left to fade away. It all came out in the wash.

Flavia went to the window. He was late. The sinking sun cast a mellow glow on the men filing up the road, the husbands and fathers who worked so hard, dull in the morning when they set off but now, coming from the pub, jolly with beer, calling out to one another, making plans. Two whole days off, most of them.

She checked on supper – the dark, rich beef stew Arthur liked, a fresh loaf keeping warm in a tea towel, butter going soft on the table. She was hungry. She usually ate with Marie at five, suppers of macaroni in gravy, boiled peas, fingerlings of cod she breaded and fried, baked potato fluffed with a fork. Marie banged the table and shouted in scribbles – not English, not Italian, nothing Flavia could understand, but Flavia always knew what she wanted.

Flavia went upstairs to check on her: fast asleep in her cot. She fixed her blankets, then went into the bathroom and put on more lipstick. Brushed her hair – it framed her face in waves, blue-black in the twilight.

It was gone eleven o'clock when Arthur finally walked through the door. He was drunk. She realized that straight off. He swayed and caught the wall. His suit jacket was buttoned wrong. He took her in: the dress, the lips, nylon stockings making a mystery of her legs. She was half afraid of what he might say – the shoes, too, were new and squeezed her feet.

He leered a bit. 'Ain't you a sight for sore eyes,' he said.

Then she was in his arms – it was real, it was happening, nothing had changed between them.

*

All weekend Flavia smiled. She looked pretty when she smiled. Marie was happy, too, or at least she didn't cry as much as she usually did when Arthur was home. Flavia served him fish pie on Saturday night, ham with parsley sauce for Sunday lunch. He was putting on weight; she wondered what he ate in London. He ate out, is what she thought, sharing a flat as he did with a friend – she could never keep track of who was who – and being unable to cook himself.

He read the newspaper, listened to 'Tampico'. He put Marie on his knee and pronounced her wet. Flavia was mortified but still she smiled. Time went too fast – before she knew it, Sunday lunch had been eaten and he wanted his suit.

As he straightened his tie by the door, Flavia finally dared to ask him, why not stay? One more night. It was a nice day. She would pack a picnic supper and they could take Marie to the bank of the Ise to see the boats. It would cap a perfect weekend, to have Arthur's head in her lap and the baby at play by her side. Flavia had dreamed just such a scene as she cooked lunch and again as she washed up, while Arthur had his nap. The sun shone into the kitchen and Flavia had been full of hope.

She asked him. It wasn't so hard as she thought, to get the words out.

He paused. He looked at her. She had Marie in her arms and the baby stared back at him: her face *his* face. Marie wrinkled her brow like she would howl, but she didn't – not a sound. They waited, Flavia and Marie, to hear what he would say. Flavia never asked anything of him. She did things the way he wanted them done, as best she could. That was her way. It was the only way she knew. Where she was from, men did not behave like this, gone from home all week, working in a city far away. No, the men were there with the family; the family was a clan, the clans led by men. Family living, like that, was deeply intimate. A routine could be established; a wife could anticipate her husband's needs, feeling him as one with sea legs feels the boat sway. A wife could be heroic, seen to be performing small miracles every day. Nearness bred such intimacy, and therein the exchange was made: what they held between them and passed back and forth, sometimes carefully, more often not. What made them cling.

Arthur smiled, thanked her for lunch, and told her that it was impossible for him to stay. He had business in London that he must attend to.

His words had the force of physical blows – they nearly knocked her down. Oh, the drag of it, the baby who would not sleep properly, eat properly, who could not do a thing for herself, who only made more work and more work, and the husband who was never home, who did not ask, when he walked through the door at the end of the week, how she was. Was she tired? Was she well? Did she need anything? He did not ask. She had never been so tired. She could not think straight, could not half organize herself to accomplish those simple household tasks she was required to undertake. The front step had not been scrubbed, nor the walk swept, no spring flowers planted or the shrubs clipped. Put the baby in the dresser and close the drawer, she had thought one day when she could not bear it another minute. The baby would be safe in there and no one could hear her scream. Flavia placed her so gently inside, the drawer lined with a blanket, and eased it closed except for a crack. Fine. The stunned silence – the relief! Then the baby started. Flavia had not even got her dust cloth in hand before the baby started. The dusting would have to wait; the baby was in her arms again and Flavia was roughly patting her back. She didn't want to hurt the baby and yet she *did* want to hurt the baby. She wanted to hurt the baby just a little bit. She pinched her experimentally. The baby stopped and looked at Flavia. Flavia smiled: she knew, the baby knew, what Flavia was up to. The baby held her breath, going purple in the face, and then she screamed. Flavia, with the wailing baby hot on her breast, looked around the room at the dust, the crumbs, the ceiling cobwebs drifting in the draught she had failed to stop up. There were mice, rats and squirrels to contend with; woodlice, in their armour, advancing from the cupboards where they mingled with earwigs in the mildew and damp. There was nothing she could do but hold that baby.

Over and again Flavia repeated the moment in other ways: she needed the toilet but the baby wept and would not be put down; she thought she would perish if she did not eat her lunch but the baby had wind. A pot overboiled. A cake burned. A bed sheet scorched when the iron overturned in her hurry to pick up the crying baby.

That Sunday, she held onto the doorframe and turned the other cheek for a kiss. The baby squirmed between them. Arthur patted Marie on the head. When he had gone, Flavia did not pinch the baby. She did nothing. She felt nothing.

She felt like nothing.

10

The lustre that once set those rooms alight had waned; silk curtains hung in ample tatters and strings; papered walls half-stripped, their raiment on the floor. Dirty windows – a long time since anything had been polished. Tarnish showed the pattern in the silver tea set still laid out in the dining room, dead flies in the sugar bowl. The telly was on in the drawing room all day and night now, for the drawing room had become a sickroom, when Sal was well enough to come downstairs, and there was an oxygen tank that hissed in one corner.

'Did you know that?' Rita asked her one afternoon as they sat together, Sal wrapped up on the chesterfield. Her hairless head bobbed when she lifted it from the pillow – such a weight to bear, now that she was skin and bones.

'Know what?'

'How much this house could be worth.'

'It's not for sale. It's not worth anything if it's not for sale.'

'You'd be rich if you sold it.'

'He would never allow it,' Sal whispered, like Arthur Gillies was in the other room and not in his grave.

'To hell with him,' Rita said. 'It's your house. He said he would give it you, didn't he? Didn't he promise? Mr Wye would have us all out on our backsides otherwise.'

Sal just shook her head.

When Arthur was tired, it was Sal who made him a cup of tea and arranged the cushions to support his back; when he caught a cold, Sal put him to bed with a hot toddy; when he sat down in a puddle, having overstepped the kerb, she did not laugh, just told the maid to wash and dry and press his clothes. She did everything to soothe him when he was cross, brewing a rum punch she knew he liked, playing 'Tampico' until the record wore out. Every week she pre-pared mutton in an old-fashioned way, with a thin slice cut the length of the leg, stuffed with herbs and butter, the slice replaced and the whole thing bound up with string and roasted and served as Sunday lunch late on a Tuesday night with potatoes and greens. On her hip she bore a scar, the ring of a dog bite from when she was a brat, but Rita always imagined the scar was where Arthur Gillies sank his teeth into Sal night after night. When it rained, she said the scar ached like the teeth were still inside. The day Sal died, mor-phine flooding her veins, she cried out in pain – she said it was like the dog hung there still, his jaw locked tight.

Sal had worked for Arthur Gillies practically all her life, from when she was very young, the most beautiful girl, but unrefined. If it weren't for Arthur she would have been a miner's wife, same as everyone else in Kiveton.

She'd had a decent enough upbringing, but mean and grey. The room she shared with her sisters was just another small room in a narrow terraced house, the hairbrush and comb on the dresser for all to use, two good dresses between three girls, nothing shop-bought except their shoes and stockings. Their father and brothers went down the pit, and so did their uncles and cousins, even the distant ones from out of the area who came to live in the pit bathhouse.

There was coal scum in every kettle of water. Black streaks in the bath and bowls, obstinate stains, as if the porcelain were scorched. Coal gritting the floorboards, crunching subtly under foot – Sal was always sweeping up; there seemed no end to it. That was life.

She went about her business in Kiveton, such as it was, until one day Arthur saw her at a bus stop and stopped his car, a smart convertible, the one he kept in a London garage full of other expensive sports cars. Mrs Peabody's cocker spaniel was sitting on the wall behind the bus stop with an intelligent look on its face, waiting, like Sal, for the bus. Arthur whistled. Sal took in at a glance his flattened nose and chalk-stripe suit, the bold yellow tie, its gleaming silk bright as new gold.

Arthur said, 'I was whistling at the dog.' He looked at her again, more carefully. 'Where are you going, love?' When Sal answered, 'Home,' he said, 'I mean in life. Are you married? Have you got a boyfriend? Because I can take you away from here.' He could talk like that, like a big shot. When he was doing business, that's how he talked.

Sal got in the car.

Mrs Peabody's cocker spaniel trotted onto the bus like it did every day for the ride home from town, where the butcher had given a bone, the greengrocer a carrot, the confectioner a bowl of water with a sherbet sweet fizzing at its bottom. Sal thought, 'Never again will I have to sit beside that greedy old dog.' The wind tangled her hair but her thoughts were clear: I won't be back, except for weddings and funerals.

As it was, once she embarked on her career she wasn't to be included in those, either. She never returned, not once, declaring London to be her soul's home. Sal knew Kiveton like the back of her hand, every street name and the way each one ran, seaming into each other like a body with all its creases and scars. She knew *who* and *what*; knew all that – the life she'd always had until she suddenly didn't – but she never went back. She didn't have the kind of mother who could forgive her multitude of sins: leaving without saying goodbye, just like *that*, with a brilliantly dressed, ugly man, to become, at his urging – the word could not even be said.

Sal pulled the car door shut and felt the leather seat unclench itself to take her weight. She forgot all about the groceries spoiling in a paper bag in the sun, the insinuating dog with its human eyes. Her family and friends would wonder where she was. Arthur handed her a scarf from his glove compartment. Knotting the scarf under her chin as she had seen women in pictures do – glamorous women, film stars and socialites and *Vogue* models – Sal already felt different. She was another girl. She was on her way to London in a fancy sports car.

On the quiet roads they talked, first in a general manner, politely, revealing more as the miles passed. Near London, Arthur told her that he had a friend waiting. Did she want to meet his friend? Sal said yes. He wanted to be sure that she understood. Yes, yes, yes. She never said no. Arthur drove her to a grand house somewhere in the middle of London – Mayfair, he said, but Mayfair meant nothing to her then – and took her inside and introduced her around. It was all a blur to Sal. Then he led her to a bedroom, lavishly furnished, where she met his friend. She slept with three more men as the night went on and the experience was not unpleasant; the men were kind to her, if ardent. She wasn't a virgin, but she was only nineteen and girls from Kiveton weren't fast.

Going to bed with Arthur was different. He took off his nice shirt and ordered her into the bath, then bathed her himself – he always liked to bathe her while the maid changed the bed. He was strong-looking, with a barrel chest and a thick covering of hair. He washed her well, soaping her all over. She had never been washed by a man before. He told her what to wear, how to style her hair, the exact shade of red lipstick he preferred. She looked wonderful in bed, he said. She looked wonderful everywhere. She would have anything she wanted.

When he left her in the morning, she was bereft. It hurt like that at first, just to be apart. She went downstairs and found three girls already seated round the kitchen table, wearing silk kimonos, two of them in curlers. One was especially tiny, her red hair pulled back with a ribbon. She smiled at Sal. There was the smell of cooked breakfast and Sal was offered a plate of bacon, sausage and eggs.

'There's bread, if you fancy a bit of toast.'

'Just a cup of tea will do me,' said Sal.

'Mr Gillies doesn't want people to think he don't feed us properly. He likes a bit of meat on our bones.'

Sal rubbed her eyes. She hadn't slept. She had no appetite, feeling as she did. Love made her stomach churn; she thought she would be sick. Those girls – they did what she had done. That's what they did.

'I'm Minnie,' the smallest one said. 'Short for Miniature.'

'I'm Louise.'

'And I'm Ava.' They smiled at her and tucked into their breakfasts.

Sal laughed, and then she cried. She couldn't say why she was crying – she was in love! But she cried all day, off and on, first at the kitchen table, then upstairs in what would be her room, face down on the bed. Louise came in at three o'clock, unwinding her curlers, and told her she'd better stop before Mr Gillies saw the state of her. Sadness was bad for business. Minnie made up a cold flannel for her swollen eyes. Ava lent a dress and some stockings and a necklace made of green stones. There was a dressing gown – a purple silk kimono – and a pile of clean linen by her bed, as well as other things they said she would need: talc, a toothbrush, a large box of condoms. No scent, they told her; high-class call girls, such as they were, never left a trail.

'It'll be all right,' Minnie said. 'You'll get used to it.'

'It's just, I was only waiting for the bus,' Sal wailed.

The bus! They laughed. It was just like Mr Gillies, they said. When he saw what he wanted, he had to have it, and he expected no less than he asked for.

'What was he doing in Kiveton?' Louise wondered.

'You know him. Always looking for new girls,' Ava said.

'Is that right?' said Sal.

'Oh, he's gone on you,' Minnie said, patting Sal. 'I've never seen him so gone on a girl before.'

They were coy as to whether they had slept with him; no one seemed to want to admit that she had not. Sal thought that if he were just there with her, she would feel better. She could do the work – she could do anything. That's how he made her feel.

Ava said not to worry, Mr Gillies was always about. He went round the houses in the evening, every single house, and there were already twelve. Then he went out. Like clockwork, he was. He stayed up all hours of the night – he loved the nightclub scene, the Hambone and the Cosmo-politan and the Colony Room. Sometimes he took a girl with him on his jaunts, just to show her off. Sal would soon see that they had got the good end of the stick when it came to these things. Minnie knew; she had worked as a hostess in Soho for Big Frank, a legendary Maltese. She said it was lovely working for Mr Gillies, even if she personally feared the man – not that he'd ever hit her, like some. It was just his way.

Frightening, he was.

Was he?

Oh, but he was nice enough, Ava said quickly. She had come to London to get on the stage – she never meant to be a call girl, only she'd been turfed out by an auntie meant to look after her. Her auntie only wanted the bit of money Ava's family sent along for her keep. 'I turned up at her door and she invited me in for a cup of tea, said she'd show me my room in a minute and did I have the thirty pound Mum gave me? Straight into her pinny pocket! She waited for me to drink up and then she said, "Right, off you go," and showed me out. She said I had to make it on my own like she did. I was only sixteen – that was two years ago. My auntie lost the job she had during the war. She got trained as a machinist but now it's the men doing everything again. Put me to the test, I'm as good as any man, says my auntie to the foreman, but he wasn't having it.' Ava added, 'I have a face for the stage. You want a bit of drama, to be an actress, and I've got that with this big chin of mine and my curly hair. Naturally curly hair, but they're not the right kind of curls so I straighten them out with the iron and then curl them up the right way.'

Louise's fellow had died in the war. She got sad when she said it and turned away, but she was soon smiling again and daubing on the mascara. She had eyes like a French actress. She thought she'd like to marry a farmer.

'Not me,' said Minnie. 'I'm holding out for a rich man.' Minnie was eighteen but she looked twelve – that was not eating enough, she said, having to go begging for her supper. Her parents were dead, and there were always ones that took advantage. She gave them a knowing look and then she laughed.

The doorbell rang. It was half past five. Minnie told them to shush. They arranged themselves on chairs around the sitting room – they called it the drawing room – before Ava opened the door to John, who seemed to know everyone. He handed over his hat and coat and she led him upstairs. Then came Frederick for Louise and, not long after that, Mr Fisher for Minnie.

Before she went up, Minnie said to Sal, 'When you do it, don't feel it. Show it, but don't feel it.' She didn't need to say. The doorbell rang. Sal opened the door.

*

At first Sal thought she was pulling a fast one on everyone who worked from nine to five, the poor sods. She really thought it was better her way, working just at night, billed as London's Bettie Page for her jet-black, extra-sharp bob. She slept late, then bathed for hours, long scented soaks that kept her limber. She oiled her skin and polished her nails. She did no washing-up. Her clothes and shoes and her evening wardrobe came from the best shops and they were well chosen, suggesting a taste not necessarily her own. Where she came from, there was no such thing as taste. What there was to buy in the shops, that was it, that was what you got: the same things everyone else had, bought with money that had been saved up, and the shops themselves were rather less exalted. But Arthur Gillies – he had accounts all over town, in Harrods and Peter Jones and the rest, and Sal simply had to walk in the door and say who she was. They were expecting her. They had things ready: elegant, expensive things put to one side that Arthur paid for.

Heads turned as she walked down the street. She was pursued endlessly. More and more men turned up at the Mayfair house asking for Sal. Arthur was no fool; he stood aside while men argued as to who had rights over others, who went first or next or last, and no one ever said it was too much money when Arthur named his price. What did they care about money? Arthur laughed when he looked at the books.

Sal had been working in the Mayfair house for nearly a year when he arrived one evening and told her to dress for dinner. They often dined together, Sal gleaming in green silk to set off her eyes, diamonds in her ears, tripping in and out of restaurants where the women, most of them respectable matrons, dressed another way: fussy evening frocks in shades of peony, fur wraps and pearls, women who wouldn't dare look at Sal. The doormen passed her a special glance: they knew all about it, and the hostess made sure of a good table.

Arthur ordered fish and it arrived with its head attached. Sal retched quietly into her napkin. She turned away and encountered cigars, bodices laced with mothballs, boiled lobsters with their eyes on stalks. A waiter passed with a tray of caviar and toast. She retched again.

Arthur flinched. He looked at her more carefully: her pallor, her shadowed eyes. The fish was removed, their coats found – Sal buried her face in silver fox fur, its softness whispering to her. In the car, neither spoke until they drew up outside the Mayfair house.

'You should have told me,' he said, not gently.

'I didn't know.'

'Well, now you know. If I know, then you know, and neither of us is stupid.'

Her eyes narrowed. 'What's that supposed to mean?'

'Don't be daft.' Then he added, 'You know what to do.'

'Do I? Because I feel confused,' she wept. 'I feel so awfully sick that I can't think.'

'It might not be—'

'What?' she choked.

'Well, whose is it?'

At that, Sal cried out, 'You think I don't know?'

'It can't be proved.'

'I'll know when I see him. When I see my boy. I already know.'

'You better go inside,' he said.

He sped off in his car, the car in which she had first arrived in town, back when she was still a girl. Wherever he went that night, whoever he was with, Sal was on his mind. She was under his skin, same as he was under hers, growing.

*

She pushed the baby out easily, in no time. Sal had always been a strong girl. The baby was a boy, just as she had said he would be. *Joseph*. She reached out her arms. The midwife hesitated; he should be washed first, she said. Sal didn't want him washed. 'Give him here,' she insisted. He immediately suckled, eyes closed, nose snuffling. He seemed to know what he should be doing, and so did she. She stroked his wet head: thick black hair, just like his father – more, in fact, than his father had on top. Sal laughed. Joseph began to shiver. 'It's that hair. Most peculiar,' the midwife said, reaching with a towel for the baby on Sal's breast. 'The wet is drawing the cold in. I better take him. Besides, he needs a wash.'

Sal refused. 'He hasn't looked at me yet.'

'He's blind anyways.' When Sal looked alarmed, the midwife said, 'Babies are, to start with. All babies have bad eyes.'

'Not bad,' said Sal, hating the midwife. 'Just not ready for the world yet.' Joseph shook with cold. The midwife dropped the towel in Sal's lap and stalked out of the room. Joseph howled when Sal pulled him from her breast in order to swaddle him – he stiffened and yelled and the whole of him turned a furious red, and then he suddenly stopped and looked at her. His blue-purple eyes, dense as a shark's, were not blind; he knew she was his mother. She felt a rush of heat and lifted the towel in time to see the high, golden arc of his stream. She laughed. He relaxed and a cooler colour returned to him. His mouth clamped down on her breast. When he finished nursing he slept, his even breathing wondrous to her. She listened to him, felt his weight in the crook of her arm: here at last.

She felt that she could never trust anyone else to look after him as well as she did and so she would not be parted from him at first. She didn't wash him, preferring instead the animal emollient that had waterproofed his skin those months he was inside her; she rubbed it in and said it did him good. She refused his place in the hospital nursery, for he would sleep with her. Sal made a name for herself on the ward for being odd and apparently unnatural, outspoken in her ways. She, likewise, could not understand the other mothers who seemed happy to be rid of their newborns. 'Poor babes,' she sighed, drawing Joseph closer.

She didn't know how they knew, but they did. The midwives and doctors and even the cleaners – they all knew. Perhaps it was the absence of Arthur Gillies in the days after Joseph was born, for he had told her he would not set foot inside any hospital. He drove her to the door in his fine car when her labour pains started and shouted for a porter. Hospitals made him ill, he said; Sal understood – she always did. Instead, she had a queue of beautiful women in daring finery and full make-up, glittering with paste jewels. She heard one midwife say that she'd seen Sal sitting in a vulgar way when the doctor looked over Joseph, and another said her dressing gown was like something for a floor show. When Minnie embraced Sal and lay down alongside her in bed to chat, Joseph between them, latched onto Sal's breast, the hospital openly declaimed against them, at which point Sal signed herself out.

She never returned to the Mayfair house. Arthur had arranged a nearby flat for her, and a nurse to take the baby when he called. He called regularly, and so did Minnie, to keep Sal company. 'Hello, handsome,' she cooed to Joseph and twirled around the room with him on one shoulder as if he were her dancing partner. If Louise or Ava were with her, they fought over who held him – Sal could see the longing in their eyes. 'Man of my dreams,' sighed Louise. Joseph was returned to his mother, smudged with lipstick and reeking of cigarettes and setting lotion. He stank of the bordello, simply put. Sal's mother would have said as much, had she seen the baby out and about and leaned into his pram for a better view, but she never did know about Joseph.

Sal insisted he had aunties aplenty to dote on him and that was enough for anyone. 'This is his family right here,' she said.

'I guess we are,' said Louise.

Joseph, in his cradle, smiled as he slept.

'Wind,' Minnie said.

'Wind,' Ava agreed.

'Oh no, this baby is happy. He's smiling,' Sal said.

'It's wind,' said Louise.

'What do you know? It's not like any of us had a baby before,' said Sal. 'He's smiling with his whole self, I believe.'

Joseph opened one eye and let it rove about, taking in the shining lamp, the silver teapot, Ava's brightly patterned headscarf covering her curlers, the cigarette moving in Minnie's mouth. There was his mother, on whom the eye came to rest. He smiled blissfully before drifting off again.

'What a miracle he is,' Sal whispered.

*

Arthur Gillies did not seem to know how to hold a baby, despite having a daughter called Marie, a bit older, up in Kettering, whom he saw every weekend. He forgot to lower his voice so that Joseph did not cry when he spoke. He banged doors. His shoes hammered the parquet floor. The hovering nurse swooped when Joseph bunched his eyes and began to shriek, exclaiming that he must be wet, tired, hungry, and off they went, down the short corridor to the safety of his nursery.

Sal tried not to think about how Arthur looked when he held Joseph: adrift, staring with a certain horror at the thing that threatened him. His beautiful suits, so carefully fitted, restricted his arms; he could not rock the baby. His silk ties spotted with posset, his diamond cufflinks caught on the extravagant lace of Joseph's blankets, unravelling his swaddling. Sal hated to see Arthur looking so lost, especially when she herself moved with new purpose and grace.

'Let's sit down,' she said to him. 'Cook roasted a joint.' For Sal also had a cook and a maid, just like a rich woman.

Arthur grunted. Sal poured him a drink and piled his plate high with pork and boiled potatoes and bright shreds of cabbage. He talked about business. He knew business, not babies. He was looking at a job lot of houses in the morning – pay cash and Bob's your uncle, he said. 'Seems like I'm the only one who's got any money to spend in this town.'

'You and the Queen. And Oxford University. I believe it was the Chancellor of Oxford himself who told me that.' Sal sipped her tea, keeping her eyes down. 'I heard Barbara from South Street is gone. And Shelley.'

'Barbara ran off with that bloke with the long hair. What's a bloke doing with long hair? Does he fancy himself a lady?' Arthur laughed.

'What about Shelley?'

He shrugged. 'Who knows? I'll let her go.'

'Ava was back at the Windmill the other day – a place has come up. She said there must have been a hundred girls there.'

'What's she doing at the Windmill? Looking for work?' he joked.

Sal nodded.

'You might speak to Louise,' he said. 'She's got to be more friendly. No one wants to hear her problems. We all lost people in the war. Always going on about finding herself a farmer.' Arthur picked his teeth. 'She's not likely to find one around here, apart from them ones that call themselves farmers but are really gentleman. Driving tractors for a lark and all.'

'Doesn't the baby look well?'

'Sure he does,' Arthur replied. He reached for the mustard. 'There's nothing in here,' he complained.

Sal threw the mustard pot against the wall, smashing it; what little mustard there was spattered the paper like bird shit.

'What's with you?'

'You're losing girls because you're not treating them right. They're good girls.'

'That's the birds and the bees for you. No one does this kind of thing forever. Girls are always moving on.' He shrugged. 'I've been around long enough to know the way things go.'

'They're good girls,' Sal repeated. 'If every girl were as good as Minnie and Ava, you'd be a millionaire.'

'Who says I'm not? You telling me how to run my business?'

'You'll lose me too if you're not careful,' Sal said, steadily as she could. 'I intend to work again, you know.'

He chased a potato with his fork, then pushed the plate away and faced her. 'Look at you. You're not the same.'

Sal knew he was right. She was a mother. She was no longer the other woman, the whore, the honeypot every man desired. Having entered the house by one door, she had left by another.

'Who'll mind the baby?'

'I will. I can do both,' Sal said fiercely.

'It's not what I was thinking at all.' He asked her for another drink. She poured a bit and corked the whisky bottle and returned it to the sideboard. She did not sit, but stood over him. She heard the nurse run Joseph's bath – how he loved his bath, and splashed and paddled, his plentiful locks curling up all over his head: angelic, he was, cherubically fat, soft and white as a powder puff.

'They ask for you,' Arthur admitted.

'What do you tell them?'

Their eyes met. 'I don't say much. I tell them you might be back one day. They say I'm a fool for losing you.'

'Have you lost me?'

He snorted.

'I want my own house to run,' she said. 'I'll pick the girls. You'll see. No one will know a better house than mine.'

Arthur sighed. He knotted his fingers together and cracked the knuckles. He inspected his fingernails. Sal waited. Down the hall they could hear Joseph shouting with delight, all sorts of babble. Arthur brought his fist down on the table.

The flat went silent and then Joseph wailed. His nurse shushed him. Sal never took her eyes off Arthur. He finished his drink. 'I tell you, it's no place to raise a child,' he said.

'I want to work. That's what I came to London to do. I'm no layabout. I want my own house and my own girls.'

Joseph, in his bath, did not make a sound. No one did. Minutes passed. Sal held her breath. Arthur began to laugh. He slapped his knee. 'You've got to turn a profit in six months.'

'I'll do better than that.'

'I don't doubt it,' Arthur said, grinning at her.

'I'll make it something special. That's what they'll say.' She'd show him – all of them.

*

She took Minnie and Ava with her to the new house in the Crescent in Primrose Hill. It was not Arthur's usual address, but she knew her customers would follow her. She liked the view from the front window, overlooking the park – which some said was just an open-air brothel anyway, come nightfall.

There was work to be done to the house, which had been damaged during the war and had a broken staircase and blown-up outbuildings spewing bricks. She instructed the builders as to how she wanted things – she would have her modern fittings, especially in the bathrooms; and electric light everywhere, even in the larder; and a double gas cooker, a fridge and a dumb waiter; and a boiler room at the back to keep the plumbing fluent with hot water. When the house had been rebuilt to the highest standard, she dressed the rooms carefully, in rich colours: mahogany and rose damask for the dining room, Delft blue in the drawing room and a soft mossy-green wallpaper the colour of American money up and down the stairs. She hung heavy drapes to make the place quiet and secret, and there were empty gilt birdcages that Sal threatened to fill with love-birds. Everywhere were mirrors, to reflect forever the good looks of the women who worked there, with whom the suitors could see themselves at play. Her brothel was elegant, costly, officiously clean, but it wasn't just that: it had Sal written all over it.

Seated fireside in the drawing room, diamonds glittering, she held court in her easy way. She read books and looked at pictures and she could always talk about what was in the newspapers. She liked a bawdy joke. Half the men came just for her conversation, or to gaze, for Sal was more beautiful than ever, resplendent in her grand house and fine clothes, never a hair out of place. *She* made the call as to who was welcome and who was not. Sal's place – that's what the concierge at certain grand hotels was asked to find. All the Hollywood actors came to the Crescent, as did MPs and high-ranking clergymen, diplomats, princes and sheiks. Her girls were appreciated as much for their coiffures and pedicures as for their bedside manner, and there were certain thrills guaranteed. Men hardly knew they were being fleeced. Every chair was occupied; standing room only. When the doorbell went, Sal herself hurried to answer – the police were handsomely paid off but she wasn't taking any chances. The neighbours never complained, not least because she gave them nothing to complain about: no drunks or noisy queues, no half-dressed women hanging out of the windows. She made sure always to greet her neighbours when they met on the street, having introduced herself when she moved in, and she was a picture of respectability, wheeling Joseph around the park in his pram, his back supported by a gold brocade cushion. She had a natty navy-blue suit just for perambulating.

Joseph's nursery was at the top of the house, next to the airing cupboard. The water pipes hissed and banged all hours but he was quiet as a mouse, Sal boasted. He drank down his bottles and never made a fuss. By day he romped as any other child would do, tumbling up and down the stairs, crawling everywhere. There were hairpins to pursue along the floorboards and an old lipstick to twist, emptied of colour, as well as the usual teddies and toy cars. Then, in the evenings, when he had been put to bed, and throughout the night – all the twelve hours that he slept – Sal crept up to him at regular intervals. He slept with his knees drawn under, thumb in his mouth; sometimes he rocked, and it stirred her, that bit of independence already, to comfort himself when she wasn't there.

Oh, but she was always there.

London was a bright blister that first summer in the Crescent, welling with yellow light. It was a happy time and Sal had all the energy in the world. She stayed up late, making money, making a name for herself, and spent the days looking after her boy in the glorious sunshine. She was safe in that house, her family with her – for she had a family now. She had Joseph and her girls, Minnie, Louise and Ava, and she saw Arthur every day that he was in town. She was blessed, she felt. She had a good life.

Making his way on hands and knees around the back garden, Joseph pointed to a snail shell. 'Dada!' He pointed to a leaf on the ground. 'Dada!' He pointed to a red rose. 'Dada!'

'Always on about his daddy, isn't he?' Ava said with a frown.

'It's just what he can say,' Sal replied. 'It don't mean anything.'

'Mean anything? When your father is Arthur Gillies it *means* something.'

Sal hushed her. 'That's enough, now.'

'It's nice having a little one around the house,' Minnie said. 'Makes the place feel like home.' She pulled Joseph onto her lap. He beamed at her, the whole of him shining and clean. 'I don't mean to stay forever, you know.'

'I expect some day we'll all be on our way to a better place,' Sal teased. 'There's still room up there for the likes of us. Just think about all those fellows who think heaven is a good roll in the hay.'

*

Sal did not allow herself to think about Arthur with his wife. The easy conversation they would have, talking over things familiar and near. They would discuss their daughter, Marie, and her behaviour, how well or not she did at school, what her friends were like, whether they were the right sort of friends to keep. When the girl needed something, her mother would ask Arthur for the money, a bit on top of her housekeeping, easy as can be. When Christmas was coming, they would plan together for the surprise.

That was the life of a family: dull, steadfast, benign, the meals prepared on time, the dirt swept up with a brush and pan, lights out by ten. It was not the life Sal wanted. Staying in at night, the wireless on in the background, a cup of tea within reach – not for Sal. She had her boy, whom she adored, but there was the backdrop of glamour as well: sequins and frills, silk, satin, cigar smoke, and night after night an ever-changing cast of characters, each with their peccadilloes.

Joseph grew and remained the most amenable child, silent as a stick if Arthur were around, but otherwise happy. Interested in buses – he spent hours in his room studying the timetables. Sal still saw in the sunrise most days and woke, after those late nights of work, in time to get him off to school. Then she returned to bed: beauty sleep was important. Housework was for the maids; Sal was a businesswoman, after all. Come afternoon, the ladies of the house were busy washing and powdering and dressing at their leisure, turning slowly before the mirror to be sure of every angle. The boy would come home from school, wanting something to eat and a cuddle. Mother is as mother does, and there was just time to sit with him while he had his tea before Sal's day, as it were, truly began.

The doorbell. Were the candles lit? Why was Annetta dragging her foot? Had she hurt herself? What was that, a bandage? What was she hiding? Who did that to you? Tell him no the next time he asks – he didn't ask? You ought to be firmer, then. Just remember, they like it when you're tough with them.

The doorbell again. 'Darling, there you are. The very man I was thinking of. Where have you been? It's an age since you were last with us! Yes, I do know it's all happening for you. Rita will take you – you remember Rita.'

It was busy like that all night. Sometimes Sal could hardly catch her breath – up and down the stairs, keeping track of the cash, pouring drinks, and then to check on Joseph and make sure he slept through it all. He always did, even when they rolled up the rugs and danced and Sal was called upon to produce alcohol and cigarettes at ever-more exorbitant prices. How they laughed, utterly careless, as the night widened and narrowed into dawn's early light.

Sal could never picture another life, but in the odd moment she did become conscious of the woman living in parallel to her, an ordinary suburban wife looking after Arthur at the weekends, raising his child, keeping house. Sal knew her name: Flavia. She was Italian – a foreigner. She lived in a quiet cul-de-sac with their daughter, Marie, and she had no idea that Sal and Joseph existed.

Sal had Arthur during the week and he went back to Kettering at weekends. That was the arrangement, and it never changed. Sal and Arthur ate together, drank together, talked and made love – he slept in her bed. She brought him a cup of tea when he woke bright and early, for no matter what time Arthur went to bed, he was always up by eight. He drank his tea, bathed and dressed and went out; he kept an office in Soho and he had his clubs as well, Boodle's and Pratt's. Arthur was always looking at houses to buy, doing things up – modernizing, he said. He kept an eye on whatever building projects were under way at the moment, dropping in on job sites; he would have been robbed otherwise. He was out all day and returned to Sal in the evening, his suits full of dust. He cleaned up again, for he still drove round the houses every night and there were fifteen now. But he always went home to Sal.

The mornings she woke with him by her side she reached for him and held him tight, and when she woke on her own he was her first thought: where he was, what he might be doing. She had borne his son. She was his heart's desire, his mistress, lover, companion and keeper, the love of his life, but she wasn't his wife. She loved him, lived for him. He was in her head all day. She always wanted to see Arthur again the moment he left. Sometimes it was all she could do to stop herself bolting the door once she had him in the house.

Nevertheless, every Friday Arthur was served a light early supper at Sal's before his car appeared out front and away he went to the station. Without fail, Sal watched him go from the window. She imagined him walking into Paddington, buying his ticket, settling himself in the first-class carriage with the *Evening Standard*, dozing on the journey and startling awake. Had he missed his station? Habit stopped him sleeping through. Then . . . what? She couldn't get beyond his arrival at Kettering. He stepped off the train, into oblivion. Into imagined bliss – except it couldn't be. He needed Sal too much for that. He'd have given up Sal long ago if it were *that*.

Sometimes she kept him on the train. Everyone gathered their things and departed but Arthur remained. He had decided sometime on the journey that he must choose. It was no good, leaving Sal every weekend, knowing how much she cried.

And yet – there was his wife, waiting for him at home. His *wife*. He had fallen in love and married Flavia a long time ago; they were married still and they had a child. He married because of the war, the first girl who caught his eye when he went abroad to fight. He'd had lovers, but not the exotic type; he thought it would be different with Flavia, that he could avoid a certain fate: becoming the same man as everyone around him. His Italian bride with her dark eyes and gentle manner, the way she covered her mouth with her hand when she spoke, as if to stop the words from coming out. She had fascinated him once, but now she wasn't even pretty. The minute she had the baby she changed. She let herself go. She aged – she looked ten years older than she was, while Sal was still a beauty, more beautiful than ever, the most beautiful woman in the world.

His choice wasn't easy. His heart was with his lover, but his wife gave him something he couldn't find words for, something that went to his core: she allowed him, in her blessed ignorance, to be the man he felt he was meant to be, the man that Sal loved. In London he was larger than life, shot through with charisma. He strutted, a bright peacock, Sal on his arm for all to see, his eyes glittering with possession. All week he flew around like that, staying up into the early hours, talking, drinking, building his business, raking in money. Then, weary, he went back to Flavia. He turned his key in the lock, swung the door wide and there it was: a gap to slip inside, somewhere to hide. With Flavia, he was just a man. She made him ordinary. He rested with Flavia. She let him be. And in the end, he was like any other man who put the bacon on the table and rolled over onto his wife on Friday night and slept a dreamless sleep until he came to in the morning.

The funeral service was in Kettering when he died. Mr Wye told Sal to stay away – it was not her day, he said. None of the girls were welcome, and if he laid eyes on any one of them trying to say goodbye, there would be hell to pay.

But that was to come, that broken-heartedness. In the

meantime, every Friday Arthur Gillies went home. He got off the train at Kettering while Sal, back in London, waited for him to return to where he belonged.

11

Sometimes she woke in the morning and for a moment she just *was*. It was so simplified. Flavia woke and it was light, or not; it was wintertime and that was something in itself, the way the dark felt, as if she had woken at the bottom of a well. Or spring had come and the curtains glowed with sunrise. Today was high summer, the sun already beating bright. Just awake, feeling but not remembering, not having a history, gathering dreams, half remembered. And, for a moment, not knowing. Feeling, seeing what it is. Country. Climate. Century. Season. What – who? Who are you? Are we together? Did she forget? Lapse in her faithfulness?

Because, if she were honest, in her dreams there were other men. Not anyone she knew or recognized, just men, young and old, nameless: a body that fed her craving, men between her thighs.

So rarely was Arthur there when she woke – now that he was dead, never, but not before, either. He was always in London. She'd got used to it and knew better than to complain; she had tolerated his working away for more than forty years, to his dying day – that kind of devotion. Her generation of women. But in Flavia's dreams it was different. All day she could put aside her longing, and then at night they came to her while she slept and was powerless to stop them. Some she wished would come again, but they never did. A new one appeared and they were naked together, doing all sorts. Things that it never occurred to her might be done – her excitement was great and she often climaxed. Then, waking, feeling the shame that came with that, Flavia prayed.

She remembered the train journey from Italy to England, just after they were married, Arthur digging under her dress and what it roused in her – desire that never went away, no matter how old she was; unsatisfied love.

He had died too soon. Flavia wasn't ready for him to go. She thought he would retire from London at a sensible age and come home to stay. They would settle into a life together. She would look after him perfectly. She would cook for him, anything he liked. They might walk around the park and stop off for a drink in the pub, he with a lager, she, a lemonade, as they had done a few times before Marie was born. He would carry her shopping. Read aloud from the newspaper. Polish an apple on his sleeve and hand it to her as if it were a gift from the very tree of life. They would watch telly in the evenings, with Marie, for she would be there, too: Gillies together.

Except that he died of a heart attack on a busy London street. She remembered the day – the doorbell rang, rare indeed, and when she looked out of the window to see who was calling, she found a policeman there. It could only be bad news. Whether it was Arthur or Marie, Flavia didn't want to know. The policeman hung around, wanting to tell her, only Flavia crouched in a corner upstairs, saying her prayers, melting into them as if a fire were in her: her visions were horrors. She wouldn't answer the door, no matter how many times the man rang. Her relief, when Marie returned at 5.30 as usual – Flavia shook as if she'd taken a chill, her teeth chattered, such joy to see her daughter. And then, knowing it was Arthur who was not coming home.

Afterwards – weeks later, when they'd taken him apart to have a good look inside – they tried to explain to her what killed him. Arteries clogged with plaque, high cholesterol, fatty diet: *her* cooking. Included in the coroner's report was the address where he'd been found. As a name and place, it meant nothing to her and so she could not see, couldn't picture in her mind the moment of his death; it was missing from her life. That she had not been there filled her with regret. He was alone when he collapsed and his death was instantaneous.

But Flavia, waking up, forgot all that just for a moment.

She woke with the taste of a man on her lips. It was light. Feeling, then seeing and, finally, knowing. She remembered who she was: wife of Arthur, deceased; mother of Marie. She offered up a Hail Mary, pushed her legs out of bed and stepped into the day.

*

Every day, Marie pretended to her mother that she went to work. She got out of the house just the same as she always did. It was already three weeks since she'd quit the Linen Cupboard. She couldn't say what exactly she'd been doing. Wandering, mostly, at first half terrified she would be seen by Flavia or someone who knew her mother – not that Flavia had friends to speak of. Neither of them did. Even so, Marie kept away from the places she knew Flavia favoured, taking the long way round if need be. She had time to go the long way. She circled Kettering, or zigzagged, entering shops randomly, handling things, buying what she liked – the usual treats and creams, but she also shopped for her holiday. She bought bright tops with short sleeves. Sandals, sturdy ones. Travel accessories, all sorts of little bits. Plugs. Insect repellent. A small travel kettle and a box of the tea bags she liked. A single teaspoon. An emergency kit full of ointments and plasters and paracetamol. Batteries. An alarm clock.

She went to the library and looked at books about Italy. She visited a travel agent – more than one. She collected brochures about Italy, sightseeing pamphlets and train timetables. She no longer had to worry about the expense – she investigated luxury hotels and spas. She studied the vistas, the arbours and vines, the masses of flowers, the turquoise waters speckled with sailing boats and speedboats and waterskiers and, overlooking these views, tables laden with food and wine. The men were handsome at every age; the women – the young women – dressed in white to set off their dark colouring, although they fared less well in later life.

Marie would need a beach towel – she bought three from Marks and Spencer because she couldn't decide which one she liked most, having the means to be indecisive now. She vowed to buy a swimming costume. She bought sun cream and a hat with a wide, floppy brim. She would sit on a beach and watch the waves roll in, a cool drink in one hand. Marie would never work again. From nine to five, Monday to Friday, she was free. The time was hers to do with as she pleased.

Sometimes she did nothing. Found a bench and twiddled her thumbs. Bit her nails. Picked at a button until it came unsewn and she tucked it into her pocket for Flavia to reattach. She devoured whole packs of gum – her jaw ached, chewing each piece only until the flavour was gone, then moving on to the next one.

Sometimes she went to the cinema – she saw every film, even the ones for children, long-drawn-out cartoons filled with catchy tunes that she found herself humming on the way home. It was a relief to get out of the sun and sit for hours on end in the cool dark. The days were hot – the heatwave – and she couldn't go home until after five o'clock.

Marie ate in cafes and restaurants, throwing away her mother's packed lunch. She took long breaks in teashops, sampling all the cakes. It was hot, so she ate ice cream and lollies, and tried sushi for the first time – she liked it, and learned to use chopsticks. Cool reams of fish and seaweed and roe that looked like jelly, salty edamame that went pop in her mouth, miso soup with melting chunks of tofu. She thought she'd like to travel to Japan – her next trip, perhaps. There was nothing, now, to hold her back.

And all the time, she was remembering. She had never gone so deep. She hadn't been interested, until now. History, before, was background, atmosphere; it was permanent and secure, moored by Flavia and the house she kept, the food she prepared, always the same: yes, *this*. The taste. The pattern on the plate. The feel of the chair. The rooms unchanged over the years. Marie had thought she would live and die that way – no, she had not thought, she had not been thinking. Not *being*.

But something had happened: she had come to be. It was a shock to her, jolting her awake. In slowly putting the pieces in place, she was making a whole – a *her*; who she was, coming together. She was here. It had been all cotton wool before.

And who was he? Who did he think he was? Who had her father been?

The weekends with him had seemed to go on forever. She thought he probably enjoyed himself, for that is what Flavia wished, to remind her father of what he missed during the week. The *peace* of home, the shelter of it. He worked so hard, Flavia said. She wanted him to rest, put his feet up, and so he did. He napped. He listened to 'Tampico' – he only wanted 'Tampico'. He wouldn't let Marie change the record, saying she'd scratch it, so Flavia moved the needle and set it carefully into the groove. Marie heard the record playing late into the night and imagined her mother dead on her feet, rolling through her hips as she sidestepped his footstool.

She remembered being scared alone at night in her room. Her mother let her keep the door open, but her father sometimes shut it.

She remembered how far away her mother sounded.

She remembered her hand on the banister going down, sliding the length of the polished wood and thinking that she would remember it always, the way she felt those nights.

She remembered it had only been the three of them, without family to speak of. No cousins, no jolly uncles, no aunts to share the burden of domestic life with Flavia, to club around the sink and talk and laugh, washing and wiping after a big meal. At Christmas and Easter, just the three of them seated at the table, heads bent over their plates – quiet, solitary days for which Flavia had prepared all week.

Flavia loved Arthur; Marie knew that she loved him. Her mother's devotion to her father, her joy when he was home – and her fear, too, that she somehow wouldn't get it right, wouldn't please him: it was all part of loving him. If Flavia felt the pinch of absence when he was away, she kept it to herself. She was that generation, the orphans and stalwarts; they picked themselves up, dusted off, carried on. They swallowed their grain of sand and the pearl formed, a glistening sac tucked inside, giving them pain. Pearl upon pearl upon pearl, knotted together on strings of suffering: sterile pain, beautiful to behold.

At five o'clock, Marie stopped, wherever she was, whatever she was doing, and turned in the direction of home.

*

Flavia heard her come in. She said a quick prayer of thanks that her girl was home safe another day, then pulled herself up from the kitchen lino, ready to greet and serve the daughter she loved more than anything in the world. Flavia cracked with every step, knees burred with kneeling, with cleaning and praying all day. Sometimes she got down and then she was stuck. She was beginning to think she ought to take her prayers in a chair but she didn't know if God allowed that. He was a loving father, but strict.

'Smells good, Ma.' Ham and peas and boiled potatoes with buttermilk gravy. Marie wiped her face with a tea towel freshly pressed by Flavia, always a clean one to hand.

'Cup of tea?'

'Please,' Marie said. 'I'm gasping.'

She drank – thirstily, Flavia noted. 'Nice day?'

Marie shrugged.

'It's quiet tonight,' Flavia said. 'Out on the street.'

'It's Tuesday,' Marie said. 'It's always quiet on Tuesday.'

'Not always. Not on Halloween. Not on Guy Fawkes,' Flavia reminded her. When Marie was a girl, Flavia could see how excited she became when it wasn't quiet. Her cheeks flushed in a becoming way – not pretty, just less sallow. She wanted to be at the window, and she didn't want the curtains drawn so she could see. Flavia would lure her back to the table only for Marie to run and look with any new pop or bang. They never went closer than that. Flavia didn't like the dark. As soon as the sun went down, she double-checked the doors were locked and automatically turned up the thermostat, even in summer. She always put the front-door light on because that was called for; to leave the light off would draw notice in the neighbourhood and she didn't want that, but neither did she expect anyone to knock at the door.

Even now, if Marie nipped out for a takeaway in the evening, Flavia fretted until she returned. Marie thought she was silly and said so – they lived in a nice area, well lit, busy enough in the evenings and then dead still, for the most part, when they wanted to sleep – but she always hurried home, not wanting her mother to worry.

The ham and peas were ready. Flavia whisked the gravy, beating out the lumps. 'You hungry? I give you a big plate, if you are. Nice big plate.' Ever since Arthur died, Flavia saved the choicest bits for Marie.

'Thanks, Ma.'

'You work hard,' Flavia said. 'I know that.'

Marie had never given Flavia any trouble. Flavia did not go through her drawers and wardrobe because Marie gave her trouble. There were so many terrible things that could happen to a girl. She didn't read the newspapers, but Arthur had told her stories, tales of horror, all about rape and murder. Innocent girls dragged off. Flavia crossed herself. Not Marie. Flavia kept her close.

*

Marie went up to bed while Flavia checked the windows and doors once more. They cleaned their teeth and kissed goodnight. In their rooms, they made the usual noises of undressing and settling in. Then it went quiet.

Marie could not sleep. She had always slept so well before; now, hardly at all. Some nights she tried to stay in bed, feeling herself to be exhausted – a frantic need to sleep and rest her fevered brain. She lay under the duvet, stick-straight, tranquillized – she hoped – by various remedies she had bought in the shops over the last few weeks, since the problem started. Nothing worked. Her knees had twinges. Her head ached with thinking and, worst of all, she had trapped wind: gas pain that couldn't be burped, a colicky baby bubble.

She must get up and walk herself about, force it out. Marie went and stood by the window. If she tried to leave the room, Flavia would wake and want to know what was wrong, for Flavia hadn't had a good night's sleep since Marie was born.

She stood for what felt like hours, looking into the night as if the answers might be writ in the sky: who, what, how, why. There was a fox hunting in their road. Marie watched him and imagined the fox knew that she watched him. Animals had that extra sense; they could hear a curtain twitch, and every footstep, inside or out – by the time a window went up an inch they were gone. The fox ran along the garden walls, jumped gates. Outside their house he always stopped and looked right at her, really looked. Their eyes met.

She had remembered, out of the blue, the address where her father was found dead on the doorstep fifteen years ago. It meant nothing to her then; she had only been to London a few times on school trips. But now – there was something familiar, some reason for it to occur to her. Sure enough, when Marie looked, it was on the list of properties Mr Wye had printed out: a house in Chelsea inhabited by one Jackie Dolk.

She made another appointment to see Mr Wye. Marie wanted to know about her father once and for all – who he had been when he was not with them, for he was not with them much. She had come to realize that they had been excluded, she and her mother, deliberately excluded, over a long period of time. There must have been a reason; otherwise he would have shared his wealth with them – shared his life.

And Mr Wye had finally admitted it to her: her father's business, his *occupation*. He had operated without partners, she was told; the army brothers didn't exist. Her father bought property cheaply in post-Blitz London and only ever used it for one purpose.

She thought she didn't hear Mr Wye correctly at first. 'Barstools?' she repeated.

'Brothels,' he said. 'The houses were brothels. High-class,' he added. 'The women were – very beautiful.'

'Brothels?' *Brothels?* No wonder he never told her mother. 'And the people who live in the houses now – did they work for my father?'

'Yes.'

Marie thought she would be sick. Old whores, that's what they were, nothing but nasty tarts. She couldn't even find the words. Her father – what he had been. She hated him. She had always hated him and now she knew why. Her father was scum. Immediately, from that moment, she wanted them gone, all of them, she didn't care how old or infirm they were. A whore was a whore, nothing more.

'Get them out,' she said. 'Those houses are mine.'

Mr Wye studied Marie: her beetled brow, shoulders rising, a solid, bullish woman in sensible shoes, ready to charge. Just like her father. 'Quite,' he said.

*

Marie was twenty minutes late to breakfast and she took her time over bacon and eggs. Her eyes with bags, dull eyes. Flavia asked her if she felt well. Marie always said she was fine. Flavia tried to hurry her along. 'You'll be late,' she said. She handed Marie her lunch in a bag and watched from the window as she set off down the road to the bus stop. Then Flavia got started, her daily adventure through the house. In Marie's room she found nothing but the usual hoard of chocolates and sweets and crisps. She persevered: behind the curtains, under the rug, a loose bit of skirting board. Nothing.

Flavia opened a window. Marie said she'd heard the heat-wave would go on all summer. That's what the forecasters said, at least – not that they always got it right. But Marie had caught the sun, for the first time in her life.

'You have freckles,' Flavia said one evening as they were washing up.

'What?'

'Freckles. You never had freckles before.'

It was true – and so were Marie's arms, wiping the dishes, brown.

How was it so, Flavia wondered?

'I eat my lunch outside. I go to the park, to get some exercise.'

That was enough, at the time, to put Flavia off the scent. Now she stood at Marie's bedroom window, looking out, feeling the change, wondering what it was all about. The sun bulged, fit to burst with hot air, like it might explode. In Italy, the Judas trees would be flowering.

12

Chocolate Bourbon biscuits were his favourite. A handful of perfect sandwich cookies he could crack open and remortar together in doubles that took his breath away. Rita was talking but he hardly heard her. Gently, ever so gently, Joseph eased the top off a Bourbon – it came free with a sheen of cream, just enough to taste.

Once, he ate twenty-nine Bourbons in one sitting, separating expertly, cream on cream perfectly joined – a real brickie, he was. Jaffa Cakes he swallowed whole, nothing to them, just a bit of air and that soft orange lozenge to nurture his throat. Ginger nuts: good for an upset stomach. Shortbread turned his mouth to paste. Hobnobs were expensive; you only paid for the name. But Bourbons – he ate a sleeve of them every Saturday night.

When he was little, Mama gave him biscuits if he hurt himself or needed cheering up; she gave him a biscuit when he had a clean plate and again before he went to sleep at night, served up on a tray with a cup of tea. But then, it was never just *one* biscuit, but three or four or five. Who could stop at one? Even the stale, soggy ones at the bottom of the tin were delicious, melting on his tongue.

He remembered when biscuits came out of a barrel. They were lucky not to have to buy the broken ones, Sal said – not like when she was growing up and biscuits were raked into a paper bag at the shop, the whole ones put to the side at home in case anyone called. No, Joseph had his pick of biscuits, and not for him the Garibaldi or a Rich Tea, the nothing ones that everybody had. Mama always bought the best, Florentines and Piccadilly biscuits that came in decorated tins. She had them sent from Fortnum & Mason.

Joseph liked a bit of cake, too. Mama didn't bake, but there were years when they had a cook and he remembered well her Victoria sponge, jam oozing from the cut, and Bakewell tart and millionaires' slices, all chocolate and caramel and a crispy bottom, rich as they come. When Joseph went out to ride the buses, he always had tea and cake with his lunch. He loved sticky brownies and lemon slices dusted with sugar and flapjack bars and meringue anything. The tea washed it down – the tea was a straightener after something so sweet.

If he hadn't had such a stutter, he might have rhapsodized on biscuits and cakes. He might have sung, or at least spoken at length. Had he been a reader of books, especially poetry, words would have come to him that named the sensations, the palate's pleasure.

He popped a biscuit in, a Jammie Dodger with a smile, the kind of thing that children ate at parties. The phone rang. It had started to ring lately, but when he answered, there was silence. He put the phone down, only for it to ring again. It rang off and on throughout the day, then nothing all night until the next morning, when it began again. It unnerved him. He tried to speak, to find out who it was and what they wanted, but his stutter always got in the way.

Joseph bumped up the volume on the telly. Let it ring. He was tired. He'd ridden the 274 end to end that morning, but it was hot and the bus was crowded, more people than ever: the tourist season had begun. Every summer, when the sun came out and the flowers bloomed, here they came, speaking in tongues, stopping in their tracks on the pavement, oblivious to traffic, often lost, just looking around, cameras going. Or they wanted a photo with their friends – did he mind? He did. He couldn't bear tourists. Sometimes he became so angry he shouted at them: fucking idiots, stupid cunts, bastards, bloody nuisance. He said it loud enough for them to hear, crystal clear. No stutter.

The phone rang. He ate another biscuit. It rang and rang. Another biscuit – another *three*, chewing faster as the ringing phone made his heart race. When it stopped, he breathed a long sigh of relief. Then it started again. He began to think that he must answer. The phone rang and rang. It did not cease.

He got up. Crumbs everywhere. Rita would fuss.

'Mr Gribble? Is that you? At last,' a woman said. 'Mr Wye would like to see you. He'll meet you at the house and he'll want to look things over.'

Mr Wye's letter was still in Joseph's pocket, soft as a rag

now, the words worn away where his fingers rubbed, reading it over and over.

'Mr Wye could be with you tomorrow.'

The biscuit tin, which Joseph had carried with him out into the hall – he could not say why – shook in his hand as he tried to get the words out. Tomorrow? What day was tomorrow? A calendar hung on the kitchen wall, but he rarely glanced at it. There was no need. Each day passed much the same as the one before, rolling along like an old dog on wheels.

'Mr Gribble?'

He cleared his throat. 'Y-y-yes.'

'Tomorrow, then. He'll be with you mid morning.' The appointment arranged, the facts agreed, Mr Wye's secretary promptly put down the phone.

*

On Tuesday Rita met Hugo Gardner for dinner. He had grown up by the sea and eaten fish every day of his life until he moved to London aged seventeen to conclude his education at King's College. He was retired from dentistry ten years now. Nineteen grandchildren – he'd had five children of his own. He said, of being a grandfather, that it was another go on the carousel. He'd been a widower six years. He had been to New York three times: twice with his wife, once on his own for a dental conference, where he walked one hundred blocks in an afternoon, from Chelsea to Harlem. A hundred minutes, which was a block a minute.

He looked around Harlem and took the subway back to his hotel. Twelve stops, thirty minutes. He had a head for figures.

'Do you now,' Rita said.

He believed in the institution of marriage. He had never strayed. His heart was true to his wife. His children, he said, thought he might find someone else now that she was dead. He needed looking after. He admitted that most men did.

Rita had been married five times. She was unlucky: her husbands always died.

All of them?

She couldn't believe it herself. She knew how it sounded. 'I'm a proper black widow,' she laughed. Mind you, she had really only started getting married in her fifties. She had been busy with her career for many years. It was hard to meet the right type in her line of work.

What sort of work was it?

'I was a companion to an older woman. I gave my whole life to her.' Rita knew how noble it sounded. 'But she passed away. Cancer.' Rita knew about cancer.

Hugo, eyes wide, took hold of his glass. 'Another bottle, I think,' he said.

On Wednesday, Frank Churchill took her out for an Italian, then pinned her to a bed in the Covent Garden Travelodge. The following weeks were quiet; the mobile phone, when she turned it on, had nothing to report. Rita didn't mind. The late nights wore her out, if she were honest. She liked her routine: sweet sherry at five, a simple supper on a tray, a whole evening of television until she staggered to bed. She came to slowly in the morning and didn't rush about, drank a cup of tea, basking in the yellow haze of her kitchen – a real suntrap, it was, especially in this heat – before she went to the house in the Crescent to see how things were. Once there, she tidied up, prepared meals for Annetta and Joseph (having got in the shopping as well) and sorted the bins and the post, what little there was – mostly flyers from estate agents who wanted the house.

There was just time for a quick cuppa and a sit-down before Joseph came back from the buses. She hardly saw Annetta, who was a hump in the bedclothes, mewling sometimes, easily comforted.

A few weeks like that: quiet, humdrum, a chance to catch up with herself and pay some bills, clean her flat from top to bottom, and now Rita was on her way to meet Colonel Smith for a drink. Another widower. 'My grandchildren tell me they don't know what the bloody hell a colonel is. They don't want to hear about old times.' He'd served as a seventeen-year-old lieutenant at the very end of the war. 'They couldn't have done it without us. The young lads had all the energy they needed to get through.' He'd gone on to make a career in the army, with postings in Aden and Abu Dhabi, where they lived like kings and queens, he and his wife. He tried to keep Rita on the phone but she told him they should save their conversation for when they met. Lonely men always wanted to talk, for which they wouldn't pay.

Colonel and Mrs Smith. It had a nice ring to it. 'My name is Richard John-Henry Archibald Smith, but my friends call

me Dick,' he had said before they hung up, leaving her with
no idea what to call him when they met. Well. She would
play it as it lay. Rita always made a good first impression. She
had on her lavender suit, the one she had worn when she
married her last husband, Terry Sourbeer. Lavender linen
and lilies of the valley to carry into the registry office, and
that bit of fancy, her feather fascinator, poking from the top
of her head, giving her another three inches – she couldn't
resist. Terry had been a tall man, and Rita was so petite.
Even with her fascinator she wasn't close to his full height.
She hadn't worn it since, and now here she was, full of opti-
mism that Colonel Smith might be the one. She wondered
if the Colonel were tall like Terry. If he were short, that
would be fine, too. Rita didn't mind.

She picked her way among the prams that crowded the
pavement. You had to be careful around so many prams; the
mothers never looked where they were going, just steamed
ahead, or swung round suddenly to charge in the opposite
direction, having remembered something they'd forgotten
in the shops. Rita's high heels pecked like chickens. She
patted her handbag. She felt people close around her,
smelled them, their toothpaste and cigarettes and curry and
garlic, washing powder, soap, their perfumes and gels and
sprays. Their size in relation to hers: how big they were, now
that she was shrinking. That was her bones drying up.
Anyone could sweep her off her feet, little as she was.

It was hot. The sun shone like the life of the party, light-
ing things up, making everything jolly. *Baking* them, an
almighty furnace. Rita wished for a parasol. She had a real

thirst on her – parched, she was. There was a pub, a place she knew, tucked out of the way in Soho. The Dog and Duck, there for years. Cool when she went in, a sort of hush, like visiting a cathedral. Rita sat with a sweet sherry. Oh, that was nice, to get off her feet.

She had another drink, keeping out of the heat. She always allowed plenty of time before a date; she didn't want to arrive huffing and puffing. She'd only put the man off. She looked at her watch. Another one, please, Rita said to the barman.

Sweet sherry made her sentimental. Maybe that's why she loved it so: it brought love back to her. She thought about her husbands, all five. It was uncanny that they had died one after the other like that, but nothing to do with her. Not *her* fault. She'd been unlucky. Ever an optimist, though, she clucked to herself, and had another gulp. Rita loved to get married. Didn't she love to get married? Didn't she just. She was Mrs Sourbeer at the moment, a name she wasn't keen on. She had been Mrs McCarthy once. Pat McCarthy worked in retail, as a shop-floor manager at Peter Jones. She married him when she was fifty-five. When she was fifty-six, he developed a mystery wasting disease and within a few months he had died, weighing just five stone. A year later she married Paul, a kindly decorator with his own business. Mrs Berndt, she was then. He was seventy-three when they married but told her he was sixty. He died six months later of a brain haemorrhage. Another one, whose name she sometimes forgot, fell from a scaffold and broke his neck looking in the windows of a house she was sure he meant to burgle.

Her last husband, Terry Sourbeer, was a real gent, but he passed on from a heart attack after a couple of years. The day he died they had been rowing, him at the top of the stairs, her at the bottom. She was ready to go out, with her hat and gloves on and a mistletoe brooch pinned to her coat. She fancied a bit of Christmas shopping, but that wasn't what they were fighting about when he dropped dead and tumbled to her feet.

'What on earth did you say?' Annetta asked.

'It wasn't what *I* said. What *he* said. He couldn't live with it.'

'Live with what?'

'He said I'd had better than him.'

'Is that what he said?'

'I'm not making this up,' Rita said.

'And what did you say?'

'Well, I was sick and tired of him saying it, wasn't I? I said yes.' Her eyes were swollen from crying. She had recovered herself with a cup of tea at the house in the Crescent, where she'd gone straight from the hospital. 'And him with his bad heart. I may as well have killed him myself. Just like a bullet.'

Terry Sourbeer was the only one of her husbands to know about Rita's past. He knew because, a long time ago, he had got himself a girl, one of Sal's famous girls, as a birthday present to himself, a gift for which he'd saved for months. He'd had to plead with Sal at the door, looking so ordinary and working-class, for she liked a referral, but she relented. Annetta tried to relax him, settling him on a kitchen chair away from the other men – men in suits who all seemed to know each other. She gave him a drink and when he'd downed it, she took him upstairs.

She was his first girl, he told her, and didn't she go and tell the others? They couldn't believe it, a real live forty-year-old virgin, good-looking enough, just a bit shy. He didn't know how to put himself across like other men, he said. He didn't know how to dance. He'd come out of the war one hundred per cent intact, and that included his cherry.

The next time Terry Sourbeer visited the house, he had Rita. He asked for Annetta – kneading the brim of his hat, his forehead studded with sweat – but she was with a Soviet agent.

'Rita here is free,' Sal said.

'That's fine,' Terry replied, hardly able to look up. He was feeling something urgent, something that needed taking care of then and there, no matter the money, which was a lot. More than he could comfortably afford twice in one month. He went with Rita, but he didn't stay the night, and after that Terry Sourbeer wasn't seen again.

He remembered her, all those years later, smiling broadly in the post office queue where they waited to collect their pensions. 'I never forgot you girls,' he told her, and there was nothing disrespectful in the way he said it.

Certainly it had happened over the years, a man coming up to her, saying she had been spectacular. A few times it happened. Not so often as she would have liked. But Arthur Gillies always said that Sal's girls were for the gods, and the gods weren't to be found hanging around Camden on a Tuesday morning.

How about a cup of tea, then? Terry knew a place around the corner. He used to work near there, in a big warehouse depot. That's how he knew about the house in the Crescent. 'It was just a normal-looking house,' he said. 'That's what I couldn't get over. You wouldn't have known it was any different from the others. If I'd seen you on the street back then, I would have thought you were nice-looking, but not a tart. Not the kind of woman I could have. But then I did, didn't I?' Terry grinned.

'Did you?' Rita asked, in genuine wonder.

'I sure did.'

'You have a good memory.'

'There were a lot of men through that house. I expect you can't remember us all.'

Rita smiled.

'The house looks the same,' he said. She nodded. 'I saw someone outside the other day. Looked like Sal – I remember her hair.'

'London's Bettie Page,' Rita said.

'She didn't look so good. She was using a stick.' He paused. 'But she didn't have any hair when I saw her.'

'She's poorly. She has cancer.'

'I'm sorry to hear that,' Terry said. He wrinkled his brow and looked at the ground. Then he blurted, 'Is it true there was a boy living there all the time?'

Rita breathed out a heavy sigh. What was the point in hiding it now? 'Yes.'

'Just imagine,' he murmured. 'A child in that house, of all places.'

'Where else was he supposed to live?' Rita demanded. 'He was with his mother. And quite right, too.'

Terry blushed. 'I'm sorry. I didn't mean – I'm sorry,' he said again, and he looked sorry, so very sorry that she felt badly for him. She hadn't meant to snap; it was habit. All those years of pretending that Joseph wasn't there.

Rita agreed to see Terry again. For three weeks they met every single day for tea and cake, and then there was a ring planted like a starry, shiny flower in the sugar bowl. She dug it out with her teaspoon. When he slipped it on her finger, Rita didn't say no.

Terry Sourbeer said more than once that he was not about to let pass an opportunity to be with a woman of her calibre, no charge, but Rita didn't take offence. He was always saying things in the name of honesty, which is just what Sal and Annetta always said about Rita, as if to excuse her rudeness. Anyway, they looked nice together, she thought, Terry with a full head of white hair and a thick moustache, his body still strong – that was forty years of lifting and moving the contents of a warehouse. And Rita, small and sharply turned out, who had shrunk in every way due to her osteoporosis, the crowded organs inside beginning to grumble and complain, her flatulence her greatest shame. Charcoal tablets were useless, she told the others, for twice a week the new Mrs Sourbeer journeyed north to the house in the Crescent and confided in her old friends.

Annetta said, 'He don't care, I bet. He's love-struck.'

'He's love-struck for a girl that's long gone,' Rita said. 'Who I am – it's all in his head.'

'We were something special, don't forget,' whispered Sal from where she lay on the chesterfield, covered in blankets.

'Now I'm just an old windbag,' Rita laughed.

'God won't mind a bit of wind,' Sal said.

'God! What do I care about God?' Rita said hotly. 'It's Terry I'm worried about.'

For a while they were happy, the Sourbeers, sharing a simple life together. He was the best of all five husbands, although she wouldn't say he was the love of her life. But he was a good man. He was gentle – a gentle giant. One of those. His pension was enough that they could dine out once a week in the curry house around the corner, where Terry bowed to the waiters and left big tips at Christmas, receiving in turn a bottle of port. They know how to look after a customer, he always said – he said it of the green-grocer, the butcher, the newsagent, the postmaster and especially the florist, from whom he bought the red sweet-heart roses that wilted on the mantelpiece the day after he brought them home to Rita. At night he whispered, 'You know how to look after a man,' but once, after too much Christmas port, he said, 'You know how to look after a cus-tomer.' Had Rita not been deep into the passive state she assumed for her married sex life, she might have replied with a strong word or two, but she often dozed while he laboured over her, or planned her shopping list, her meal rota, what she would wear to the curry house next time.

'I'm too old for this,' she told Annetta one day. 'I'm like

a crab, with my bones so stiff around me. I get the hot-water bottle first, to loosen me up, then Terry does his thing, then I want the hot-water bottle back and I want it fresh and hot so he's got to go down to the kitchen just when he's exhausted himself.'

'He may as well make you a cup of tea while he's at it,' Annetta said.

'Oh yes, and that. So he does, just the way I like it, not too strong, half a teaspoon of sugar and plenty of milk,' Rita said, and they laughed. It was always grand to laugh about men. It seemed a long time since they had laughed like that.

Rita sat in the Dog and Duck and laughed to herself. Her fascinator jigged a merry little fairy dance. Richard John-Henry Archibald Smith – what a name. Call him Dick. Never mind. A man was a man was a man, in Rita's book.

*

Joseph remembered him. There were certain ones, regulars, the faithful and devoted, and then there was Mr Wye, who seemed to be always around the house. His father joked that Mr Wye was in love with Mama – he joked, but his tone was a warning, and Joseph noticed that Mama was all business when Mr Wye was there.

His mother and father's love was not to be disputed and yet could only be alluded to. Joseph knew his father was married to someone else and there was a child, a girl, not much older than he was. He knew because he listened, legs going dead in a cupboard – not because anyone told him.

Mama tried to talk to him about it in her own way, which was to be nice and not say anything that hurt. Joseph knew his father didn't love him. What was important was that Arthur loved Mama. That's what it was all about.

Joseph had seen men come and go from his window. He heard, from behind a door, men cry out in different ways. He remembered voices. There were certain ones he knew, even if he never put a face to the man. The way they carried up the stairs – the voice of success, the self-made millionaires, everlastingly bombastic, and the gnarled tones of the upper class. Some men cleared their throats before they spoke or even when they thought of speaking. Others repeated themselves – every time the same stories. There were one or two stutters, carefully disguised, and the odd lisp, and the curious effect of a cleft palate.

The doorbell rang or there was a knock. Men in the front hall, Mama ushering them through to the drawing room, laughter like braying donkeys. Mama dashed here and there – she ran up to her bedroom, where the safe was, and back down again, having checked that the bathrooms were clean. She called out the drinks – gin and tonic for Mr Webster, whisky for Mr Roget.

Joseph heard film scripts and speeches, some of them later to be famous. He heard the sound of feet running up and down the stairs the night the actor dropped dead on Annetta; he had watched from his window as they bundled the body into a car that sped off into the dark.

He knew there was drunkenness, hearing how the noise grew as the night wore on. The bawdy jokes his mother told, her potty mouth, drawn in red. Her lipstick did abound on the faces of those who visited her house, although she was the picture of innocence if ever Arthur quizzed her, saying she was only being friendly; Arthur could be jealous. Mama pointed out that it was good for business, and when she took that line he didn't argue with her.

Joseph remembered there was music, of the kind that Rita called hoochy-koochy – Arthur liked 'Tampico' to his dying day. Sometimes there was dancing, when Annetta closed her eyes as if dreaming and laid her head on the shoulder of her partner.

He heard them weep, all the ladies of the house. Even Rita. He heard her more than once, on her own in her room, her tears mixed up with words he couldn't make out. Mostly she cried when she was drunk. She cried into her pillow and then she moaned as if someone else were in there with her when he knew she was alone.

Joseph knew everything that had gone on. Of course he knew. It couldn't be kept from him. He was always going to know. They were lucky to do so well, Mama said, later, when he was older and could understand. It seemed as if it would go on forever, the house as it was then, not the house as it was now, flaking paint, the floorboards spitting nails, the rugs full of holes – moths and stiletto heels and years of hard wear, heavy traffic in and out of the front door. Buckets everywhere, to catch the rain coming through the roof. The bath enamel had worn away and the taps dripped, forming stalactites of limescale. The front hall ceiling came down one day so that the floor joists overhead showed, a skeleton hung with shreds. Who would want it? Who else could ever live there?

His thoughts carried him along on a bedevilling river that ran and ran and ran.

*

The man behind the bar called it a goblet. It was a goblet she was after. A goblet of sweet sherry, please, she said to the man, and that was gone before she knew it, so she had one more. A fellow came in who reminded her of Arthur Gillies. He looked around quickly, winked at Rita and left. It was the set of his shoulders that made her think of Arthur – built like a bull.

She remembered how he let his eyes sink into her. She gazed back, unafraid, until he looked away. She used to stare him down – she loved to make Arthur blush. As far as she knew, he didn't blush for anyone else, not even Sal.

Arthur Gillies wanted Rita from the moment he laid eyes on her at the Colony Room, back when she was the coat-check girl. She tried to get off with him then but he put his tail between his legs and ran to Sal, who sat in rapt attention on a banquette, watching the band, up to her ears in silk and sables. When they met again in Sal's drawing room, his eyes lit up. You.

They were always preening at each other after that. He didn't sky-point his great bill of a nose just for Sal; he did it for Rita as well. He took more care in his dress and tried not to eat so much. He looked after his teeth. He fussed with his hair to hide the bald spot. He caught Rita's eye and smiled. He enquired, when they met, how she was, meaning how she felt about him. Was it still on? She smiled. It was on. He looked across a room full of important men to see if she were looking at him. Was she his? She was. She didn't want anyone else. They had their own language; they had made their bond. They knew each other without speaking. For all of Sal's talk of her sixth sense with men, she didn't sense Arthur Gillies wandering off – but Rita did. She knew he dreamed of her in his bed. He loved her as well as loving Sal and sometimes he loved Rita more. There were whole years he loved her more.

She waited. She thought he would come to her. She created opportunities to be with him: they met on the stairs, in corridors, the front hall, and Rita thought her heart would burst. She could hardly speak sometimes – she, Rita, speechless! He was the kind of powerful man who could change the temperature in a room, making everyone excited; and who spoiled things if he felt like it, if he were in a bad mood. She listened to every word said about Arthur and stored away the information, building a fuller picture of him in her head, loving him more and more. She learned when to expect him at the house, being, as he was, a creature of habit, and when he did finally arrive she always looked her best. Then she would take in his pupils' dilation, the delight of seeing her there. Every time they met they renewed their bond; he happened to her all over again. It made her wild. There were times she thought she would die for wanting and not having Arthur Gillies.

Sal was practical about the good looks and physical allure of the girls who worked for her. It was what the job called for, and Rita had proved herself a star. She bloomed with the luxuries her life afforded her, the easy hours, the soft carpeting that ran through the house and cushioned her joints, overstuffed furniture on which to drape herself into alluring shapes. The food was good, prepared by an expert cook, and just before dawn Rita would curl into a small parcel and replenish herself on the deepest mattress Harrods sold. Arthur saw how well she looked on living in his house and it pleased him.

She felt his eyes on her all the time. When he could steal a moment, he drew up beside her, idled a while. She held her breath as they stood together, very close, looking at each other, doing nothing. Rita loved him. She had always loved him – loved him still. No other man was half as good. She could have kissed him. If only she had kissed him when she had the chance.

Another sweet sherry, then. Who was she to refuse the offer of a drink bought for her? She smiled at the only other customer in the Dog and Duck, an ancient mariner, pure wreckage, wrapped up in a shabby coat and hat – despite the heat. Rita raised her glass and toasted him, but privately she drank to Arthur Gillies. He was in his grave and she would live forever. She'd live to be a hundred, at least, and get her letter from the Queen. *That* was something to hang on the wall, just the kind of thing to make Sal green with envy. If only she had lived to see.

Rita remembered the look on Sal's face when she

announced that she would marry Pat McCarthy, who had wooed her quietly for six weeks before they booked in at the registry. They were to marry the following day and Rita was upstairs packing her case. A new dress from Peter Jones, a sheath of ivory shantung, hung in the wardrobe, and when Sal came in she admired it.

It was then that Rita told her, having not breathed a word to anyone until that moment. Her heart had been true to Arthur Gillies for so long that she never considered loving another. Besides, he could be terribly jealous. When she went upstairs on the arm of a punter, he always looked the other way and set his jaw, as if to bear it.

How long had that dance of theirs gone on? Twenty years? Thirty? She wouldn't have said it was a complete waste of her life, loving Arthur, who would never come to her, who did not intend to leave his wife *or* his mistress; who would not give up his kingdom, not for her. The old fantasy, where he carried her off in his arms to make a new life together somewhere – no, she wouldn't wait another minute for Arthur Gillies! She didn't have *time* to wait. Rita knew she had to get out fast if she stood any chance. Business at the house in the Crescent wasn't what it once had been. They were down to a handful of loyal gentleman callers by then. They didn't have the maids they used to, or the cook, and Joseph was all grown up. Even Arthur wasn't around much, spending his time elsewhere, in other houses, where the younger women were. So when Sal said of Pat McCarthy that she didn't think it was enough time to know someone properly, let alone marry him, Rita threw back at her, 'How long do you plan to wait on Mr Gillies?'

Sal stroked the wedding dress. She didn't speak. Annetta was upstairs with someone, an old faithful, making an awful ruckus, and Joseph was out riding the buses. Sal said, 'Arthur is already married.'

Rita snorted. 'Well. I know that. But I wouldn't put up with it.'

'Put up with it? Put up with what? I have the best of both worlds. Who wants to be a wife? Always nagging him about this or that. Not for me, thank you.' But Rita knew Sal would have married Arthur if she could. Rita, too. She would have married Arthur Gillies at the drop of a hat, but he never asked her, either.

'He hasn't been here for three nights,' Rita had said to Sal, and she was not sorry to say it. She'd heard that Arthur was in love with a French girl who worked in the Chelsea house. *La Gorge*, they called her. *La Gorge* had him under a spell. The younger girls, they did everything.

La Gorge.

'Business,' Sal muttered. She looked haggard. Her eyes crinkled when she grimaced at her hands: jewelled fingers, minus a wedding band. Still, she lingered while Rita packed her case, not saying much, both of them praying for the doorbell to ring and burst the tension. It never rang. Then Annetta finished upstairs and the gentleman bade them a jolly farewell, for they were all friends, having known each other for many years. Joseph came back from riding the buses and they sat down to supper, which Rita had prepared, as usual. After supper they gathered in front of the television, where they spent most evenings, dressed up just in case. Sal listened for the door, for Arthur's key in the lock or a knock that meant a punter was waiting. None came.

'Never mind,' Annetta said.

Sal didn't say anything, just tried to enjoy whatever programme they watched. Without Arthur, she had lost her power, her spark. To have a television in the drawing room was a step down; there was no opportunity for conversation when the telly was on, she always said. The men she knew, the men who came to her house seeking excitement or comfort, were for the most part big talkers, especially about themselves. It was part of the service. They needed attention, that's all.

At midnight Sal rose and switched off the telly. She pushed the deadbolt into place. Arthur was not coming – no one was. Even so, she left the light on. Just in case.

When they bade each other goodnight, they always kissed on the lips, like real sisters.

'Goodnight, then,' Rita said.

In the morning, she rose early to bathe and dress with care. She made up her face, fastened on pearls – a wedding gift from Pat McCarthy – and sprayed her black curls into a stiff filigree crown of sorts. Her dress showed off her narrow frame; Rita hadn't gained an ounce since she was twenty, she always boasted. When she went downstairs, Sal asked for her key and Rita gave it. Later that afternoon, after a drink or two to calm her nerves, she married Pat McCarthy, who knew nothing about her past as one of London's famed prostitutes, and that was the end of *that*.

Rita had better be off. Colonel Smith awaited her at a table for two around the corner.

What was this business of her not being able to stand up properly?

It might have been five goblets. Sometimes Rita lost track, but that wasn't her memory going, it was just her enjoying herself. She was sharp as a tack. She emptied her purse onto the table: a few pennies, a ten-pence piece. She had spent it all. Good thing she had her bus pass.

Rita knocked over her chair. Eyes on her. The ancient mariner. S'funny. She was a picture in her lavender suit and feather fascinator. Dear Lord, put out a hand, someone, for here came a black wave, rushing and boiling, fizzing in her ears, and it swept her from her feet.

*

When Arthur died suddenly, Mama went into shock. She was hysterical from the moment she heard in a phone call from one of the girls at the Chelsea house. Something about his heart. Rita had taken the phone when Mama began to scream. 'Tell me,' Rita said into the receiver, and when she was told, all colour drained from her face.

'You won't like this,' she said, turning to Joseph. 'Your father's dead.' It might have been the first time that Rita referred to Arthur Gillies as Joseph's father. The truth was always in the air, but even so was never stated loud and clear.

Mama closed the doors to the Crescent house immediately and took to her bed. When Mr Wye forbade her to attend Arthur's funeral, she threatened to kill herself. How she wailed as the hour of the service came and went and his body was put into the ground. She wanted death in those first months of grief. She could hardly bear to look at Joseph, who resembled his father so much. Sometimes she shut the door on him and wouldn't see him for days on end. It broke his heart, to be pushed away like that.

Joseph cowered in his room. Mama was Mama, irreplaceable, and he wanted her desperately. He hated Arthur Gillies all the more for this last trick. His father – yet Arthur had never been a father to Joseph. Joseph felt no acknowledgment, no *affection* from him, just the grim, granite look whenever Arthur glanced in his direction, and the way he always wanted all of Mama's attention when he was in the house. Forty years of that: Joseph was glad he was dead.

But Mama's grief was slow to give; the noose was tight. For a long time all was black before her eyes. It was months before she properly embraced Joseph, and his face, so like his father's, ceased to make her cry.

After Arthur died and the houses were officially closed, there was no need for Mr Wye to call, although he still dropped by from time to time for tea with Mama. 'Your mother and I need to have a word,' Mr Wye would say, and Mama smiled at Joseph as if to reassure him all was well: a nervy smile that made her cheeks tremble. Joseph always toddled off straight away to find a quiet spot to eavesdrop. Mostly Mr Wye talked business: long, dull conversations that made him yawn. He also tried to kiss Mama more than once and she was always politely firm in her refusal, reminding him of her status, if not her title.

It was only when she became ill that he stopped his visits. After she died, Mr Wye simply disappeared. There had been no communication from him since, in six years – and now this. Mr Wye was coming tomorrow.

Joseph's asthma – the orchestra arrived. Tuning up: strings, then wind instruments, one on top of the other, and a timpani. Ribs of iron – they would not give; a vice, an almighty screw. When he breathed he crucified himself.

Breathe not.

The phone rang. He heard it as if from a distance. To breathe, he needed his inhaler – not there when he felt in his pocket. He called out for Annetta. His stutter. Breathe not. He clamoured for air: not there. The letter from Mr Wye – not there when he felt in his pocket.

The appointment tomorrow.

The phone rang and rang. Joseph picked it up but his efforts to speak were useless. He clawed at himself. Wings beat in his ears. Soon he lost consciousness.

*

Next thing she knew the driver was shaking her awake outside the house in the Crescent.

'Black waves,' she said to him, by way of explanation.

'Will I help you to the door, madam?'

'Oh, for goodness' sake,' Rita said. Annetta stood on the

front step, wearing her underpants over a pair of trousers – Joseph's grey flannel trousers – and nothing else. The taxi driver sniggered. Rita shot him a look. 'Pray you don't get what she's got.'

Annetta seemed not to recognize Rita. She smelled strongly of urine; she was wet down her front. 'Joseph!' Rita banged on the door. Where was he? 'Open up, Joseph!' She couldn't make the key fit. It wasn't the right key. She tried again, and again. When she finally got the door open, there was Joseph, down on the floor.

The *storm* of him, lungs full of rain, every last gasp flattening into fizz. Beads of sweat stood out on his forehead like hail pellets – soaked through, he was, but no wind to fill him up. Annetta pestered him with questions. What was he doing down there? Was he sleeping? Was he tired? She joined him on the floor – she had caught sight of the biscuit tin lodged under one leg. The tin was crushed, bent out of shape; a tin that had been with them since the old days. Its lid would not fit, no matter how Annetta wept and pressed – she had the tin on his chest and was putting her weight into it, pressing for England, pushing the life out of him.

Rita barked orders that no one heard or understood, her feathery fascinator pointing fingers in all directions. 'Annetta, hurry and get his – upstairs – no, leave the tin. Leave the tin, I said. Leave the bastard – go on! Go *on*. Hurry up now, darling, Joseph needs his – his – his thingy. His thing to breathe. Annetta! Do you hear me?' And off Annetta went, taking the biscuit tin with her.

Joseph spluttered, his face like a boiled cauliflower:

waterlogged, colourless. He tugged at Rita's sleeve and then his damp hand slid down her arm. Rita fanned him, as if that would help get the air in. Annetta reappeared, empty-handed, at the top of the stairs.

'What?' she said.

'His – to help him. His *thing*. His blue inhaler.' Rita finally found the word. 'His inhaler,' she repeated triumphantly.

Annetta left and returned, bearing the biscuit tin.

Rita rolled her eyes to the ceiling. 'God give me strength.'

'Why is Joseph on the floor?' Annetta said, coming down the stairs and bending over him. 'Have you fallen, Joseph? Did you hit your head?'

Rita lurched to her feet. She would get it herself, just like she always did. In her good wedding suit, too. Chasing rainbows round the house, fetching things for them. Oh, it made her cross, the way she waited hand and foot. And then she saw it: Joseph's inhaler in a dark corner of the front hall. 'There,' she cried, and she had it, sticky with cobwebs. 'Right here all the time. What are you like, Joseph?' She inserted the inhaler into his mouth and squirted. 'Feel his feet. Like ice.'

'Is that very bad?'

'Let's warm him up.' Rita peeled off his socks. 'Annetta, the other one.' Annetta did the same – maybe it came back to her from all those years ago, how to touch a man and make him come to life in her hand.

The medicine took hold and eased Joseph's chest. He breathed. His colour returned. Rita helped him to the chesterfield, tucked him in with a rug despite the day's heat. She went downstairs and boiled the kettle, reappeared with a laden tea tray. The biscuit tin was passed round for inspection. No, they couldn't believe the state of it. 'Like an asteroid hit,' Rita declared. 'All bent out of shape. There's nothing a soul can do with it now. Look at her shoulders, poor girl.' Sure enough, the young Queen seemed to stoop under the weight of her ermine.

'We'll never find another one the same,' Annetta added mournfully. 'It was a Peek Freans. Remember the picnic we had on the day? Joseph, you were only tiny. We went across to the park and had coronation chicken sandwiches and sausage rolls and potted shrimps and lemonade and a tin of Peek Freans. I still love a Bourbon biscuit – just like you, Joseph. Always my favourite. It was what my mother called a proper biscuit. A Bourbon biscuit was a Sunday biscuit.'

'Gracious me! How you can remember all that and not remember the blooming way home, I'll never know,' Rita said.

Joseph's fingers played with the fringe of the rug. He remembered the picnic – so unusual for them to have a day out together, mixing with people as if they were just the same. He sat close to Mama, watching the other children. There was a blaze of sun. When Mama pushed him to join in the play, he cried. She had looked at Rita and Annetta and sighed, then offered him a biscuit. By the end of the day he'd got the tin on his lap, having his fill while the games went on. But then it never was enough biscuits, not even when Joseph scoffed the lot, not for the hole *he* had in him.

His eyes glided about the room, catching on antimacassars and cushions that had lost their feathers, the tarnished silver and filmy crystal decorating the mantel, the familiar pictures hung askew. He heard the fire click as it flared and waned, another old thing on its last legs but still going. He was alive. He could see, hear, touch and taste – he ate another biscuit, washed it down with tea. He could speak, but they would only talk over him.

'Joseph needs another cuppa,' Rita said. 'Never mind me, I'll take what's left in the pot. I don't mind the dregs. You look like you've been in the wars, Joseph. What a day.' It was clear to Joseph that she was drunk, reeling as she was, dropping things, rattling the cups in their saucers as she passed them round. He had smelled it on her breath when she tucked him into his nest on the chesterfield – a wine of some sort, sweetly fermented.

'I want sugar,' Annetta said.

'Of course you do, darling,' Rita said, stirring it in. Finally, after much fussing and stumbling, she sat.

In such a life a biscuit tin becomes a beloved friend. As they passed the tin, they spoke of it fondly, commending its service: fifty years of biscuits. Annetta stroked the Queen's faded cheek, then Rita took the tin and placed it on a high shelf above the telly, looking out over the room: Elizabeth, newly crowned, right hand raised to acknowledge her subjects.

'There she is,' Annetta said. 'Doesn't she look marvellous? She's just the same as us, you know.'

Rita snorted. 'Like hell she is.'

Then Rita said she might have another tin to spare at

home – Quality Street, mind, but perfectly adequate, one of their jumbo Christmas tins that she loved.

'I'm a chocoholic,' Annetta declared. 'Oh yes, a chocoholic,' she said happily. 'That's me.'

'I like a toffee,' said Rita. 'When was the last time you had a toffee?' And she tipped back her head and opened her mouth as if to let the syrup pour in and set her teeth as solid as in concrete.

Annetta laughed and clapped her hands in delight, and even Rita was smiling. Joseph snuggled under his rug. No one saw them, but they were there. They had been there all the time.

13

Marie stopped at a phone box, as was her habit now. She used them all around town, so as not to leave a trail. She swiped her calling card, dialled a number. The line connected – it *tugged*. A woman answered, sometimes a man – one man, not so old as the women. He had a stutter, that's how she remembered him. The women sounded uncertain. It wasn't hard to scare them. She didn't *say* anything, and the doing was easy enough: just pick up the phone; any phone would do. Dial, take a breath and hold it. *Hello? Hello?* Marie heard their growing fear, the breathing at the other end becoming more harried: catching on itself like a record that skipped. But she never spoke, never reassured them that all would be well, for these people lived in her houses and she intended to sell: the money would be good. The money, on twenty houses, would be great – she, who was already rich, would be richer by miles.

Eventually both parties put down the phone. Try again, another one, or the same helpless person. All day long.

That's what Marie did now. It killed the time until she could go home.

She dialled. Listened – as long as it took. She was not having fun, doing this. That's not why she did it. She was having her revenge. Those women – in her houses – what they had done. Slappers! Whores! Living off the fat of *her* land. Marie wouldn't stand for it.

*

Egg and chips for supper, double-dipping the potato wedges in boiling fat to crisp them up. The way Flavia fried eggs, throwing a little water into the pan after the white had set; the water bubbled instantly, lifting the white, flying-saucer-like, poaching it. 'I love this supper,' Marie said, adding salt and vinegar and ketchup to her chips, prodding the yolk until it burst, a hot dip that would cool and harden if she wasn't quick.

'So simple,' Flavia said. 'An easy supper on a hot day. Who wants to cook in this heat?'

Marie ate heartily. She described, over the meal, the new linen that had arrived in the shop, all tropical floral sheets and napkin rings made to look like gilt braid and the beach towel that was all the rage, printed with a waterskiing penguin.

She helped her mother with the washing-up and went off to watch telly.

Flavia's hip juddered as she lowered herself onto the hard floor to pray. She crossed herself, saying a quick one just to get herself down there. When she thought she needed to do a bit of penance, she removed the bedside rug or knelt, as she was doing now, on the kitchen lino.

Dear Lord, she had been in her daughter's wardrobe again, to see what was new, what was hidden.

Ave Maria, gratia plena, dominus tecum.

She used the worktop to pull herself up. Back on her feet, she didn't like to sit down again until she knew she was done. Checking one last time that the kitchen was tidy – she found crumbs on the table and dabbed them away with a moistened fingertip – Flavia hobbled off to join Marie in the sitting room.

She looked at her daughter on the couch.

'What, Ma?'

'More sun,' Flavia said. 'On your face. More brown.'

'I told you, I sit outside when I have my lunch. It's too hot in the shop. What do you want to watch?'

'Anything,' Flavia said. 'I'm not fussy.' She patted her belly. 'I don't think I could eat another thing.'

'But I have a treat,' Marie smiled.

They watched television while they picked over the box of chocolates that Marie produced from upstairs. She never failed to produce a box of chocolates in the evening. She had a stack of them in her wardrobe, all Thorntons, big boxes of truffles, extra sweet. Flavia turned up the central heating – even in that hot weather, when she and Marie steamed like puddings.

They sat there until bedtime. They had tea and biscuits – last food, Flavia called it – then she gathered the cups and saucers and took them to the kitchen, leaving them by the sink; it was a privilege she allowed herself, to leave these few dishes until the morning.

Marie suddenly went to her mother and put her arms around her and kissed her – so tender. Flavia was surprised. It was a long time since they had touched each other, despite living together all those years.

'Goodnight,' Flavia said, wiping Marie's cheek with a finger. Drying it.

'Goodnight, Ma.'

*

Everything was ready; her suitcase was packed, holed up in a locker at the railway station. She had double-checked her tickets and itinerary – she had the details memorized, her brain having proved itself capacious for facts and figures, now that it was properly engaged.

After supper, once they'd washed up, they watched a bit of telly. Marie could do that without really being there. She could sit with her mother, *fill her chair*, for all Flavia wanted was some company; the ghost of a person was enough. Marie laughed when Flavia laughed. They shared a box of chocolates. Marie offered to boil the kettle but Flavia shook her head and set off to the kitchen. 'You want a biscuit?' she called. Marie always did.

Marie had already sent Flavia a postcard – from Kettering – which would be the first of a series, for she intended to write to her mother every day she was travelling, as well as taking photographs and keeping a journal. She would be gone for three weeks, she wrote in plainest English. She was going to Italy for a holiday. Sorry to tell her mother this way. Then she explained where Flavia would find a copy of her itinerary, plus the person to call in case of any questions or emergencies: Thomas Wye, followed by his number – although Flavia was unlikely to call, for Marie didn't remember ever seeing her pick up the phone. If Marie were at home, Flavia made her call whoever it was she needed.

The postcard was on its way. Everything that would come to be had begun. She did not expect Flavia to *die* of the shock, but there was always the risk with old people.

*

All night Flavia prayed. Marie was up and down to the toilet – when they met in the hall, she reassured her mother that she felt fine.

'There's nothing wrong with me.'

'But are you sleeping?'

Marie shrugged. 'The same.' She burped. 'Excuse me.'

'That feels better. Does it? Is it a bubble in there? Some wind?'

'No, I'm fine.'

'A tumour, do you think?'

'Don't be silly. I don't have a tumour. Go to sleep, Ma,' Marie said, bestowing another kiss upon Flavia.

But Flavia didn't sleep. She listened to Marie moving

around her room for hours, opening and closing drawers, but in such a way as to be trying not to be heard. Just before dawn, her daughter must finally have slept, for the house went quiet. Flavia got up and made Marie a cooked breakfast – everything, the works. Sausage, bacon *and* black pudding. Grilled tomatoes and fried mushrooms, fried bread, toast, baked beans in a mug. While Marie ate the lot, she prepared her lunch: pasta salad, fruit salad, bread and cheese and a slice of coconut cake, carefully wrapped in foil.

Marie paused at the front door, then suddenly turned back to kiss Flavia – a third kiss, unexpected. Flavia didn't know what to say.

'You'll be late,' she said.

'Bye, Ma.'

'Have a good day.'

'Yes, Ma.'

She watched Marie go until she disappeared from view. Perhaps she looked a bit sturdier than usual. She had purpose to her step. She seemed more confident of late, Flavia had noticed, and her suntan suited her.

Flavia immediately retrieved her cleaning things and went upstairs to Marie's room. It was Wednesday – not her usual day to do the bedrooms.

She felt it the minute she walked through the door: the feeling of things being disturbed. Marie's room had been recently ransacked and put back together again. But not by Flavia.

And—

Things had been hidden, of that she was sure.

Then she found, in Marie's top dresser drawer, a large brown envelope stuffed full. Flavia tore it open and its contents spilled on the floor. She didn't care about the mess, for once. She knelt, as if at prayer. It took a long time to go through all the material, which included pamphlets and brochures and train timetables, much of which she couldn't read, being written in English, but the station names were familiar. Marie was off on a big trip to Italy, leaving that day. She would be away for three weeks.

At first Flavia still tried to clean, but she was clumsy, for she was weeping, and she soon gave up and went downstairs to sit. Flavia faced a weary, desperate time until Marie's return, like a desert to cross. Even prayer was just another chore to struggle with, although she prayed regardless. There was no peace, no joy, for now her prayers would not be answered: that Marie be returned to her safe another day.

She sat and waited, only half believing that her daughter was not coming back. She prayed, how she prayed! She did not wash up the breakfast dishes and had no appetite for lunch. The minutes dragged; she watched the clock, always surprised by how slow it was. Flavia didn't think she could stand it, time at that pace – not for three weeks.

When 5.30 came and went and there was still no sign of Marie, Flavia knew for certain that she would not be home that evening. She remained sitting, praying, weeping, until it was dark; then she went and turned on the front porch light and returned to the couch.

Deus meus, ex toto corde paenitet me omnium meorum peccatorum.

She remembered when Arthur died: when she stopped waiting for him to come home.

14

The kitchen light, when he switched it on, blew with a bright pop, giving him a shock. Joseph stepped into the dark. He knew just where to go, which cupboard to grope. No biscuit tin, not any more, but there were packets. He would tell Rita about the light bulb; she was the one who took care of things like that.

He'd sneaked downstairs just to get away from them. Sometimes Rita used up all the air. It made him need his inhaler, and he'd had quite enough of that for one day, thank you. Joseph wasn't right yet, after his profound attack earlier that afternoon, but he was better than he'd been then. For a minute there he'd thought he was a goner.

It was cool in the kitchen. Cool and smooth, the lino floor – he felt like getting down to put his cheek to it, so hot upstairs and him smothered under a rug all afternoon, for Rita wouldn't let them open the windows and doors lest Annetta hop out and disappear. Rita had everything locked up tight – she had wobbled around the house making sure, leaning on walls to steady herself, bumping into the furniture. It was a long time since Joseph had seen her drunk. He remembered when she used to disappear on benders, gone for days on end. Mama was always furious. But Rita got the trade in and got everyone drinking more than they should, which made money, and although Mama complained bitterly about the situation, she never let Rita go. They were sisters, Mama said, to the end. They fought like cats and dogs, too, but that was to be expected in a house full of women sharing clothes and men.

Joseph, in the dark, carefully, meditatively stacked biscuits, lining up their edges. He felt the weight of the pile in his hand and wondered if it would be enough. Then, one by one, he put the biscuits whole into his mouth, gossamer butter galettes that tasted like soap. He wondered why Rita bought them, but from time to time she did, fragile French biscuits that broke the minute they were out of the package. Mama had a thing against French biscuits. She said, 'I hate their thinness. They stick in my throat. Makes me feel as though I can't breathe.'

He doubled them up, two at a time instead of one. He crunched them into suspension, sucking air through his nose in greedy snorts, his mouth packed full, nothing else, no other thoughts. *So good.*

Upstairs, the phone rang. He froze. He listened to it ring. He did not want to answer, knowing the caller was likely neither to speak nor to hang up until he did. Always the same caller, Joseph was sure; sometimes he heard them sigh or sniff, but otherwise they were silent, and this silence was a burden to Joseph, a punishment. Whoever it was, they were vicious; he sensed their rage. The caller had something against him. If only he knew what.

Rita was by the front window, where she always liked to stand. She stood as if she had a drink in one hand. She heard the phone ringing in the front hall and went to answer. 'Hello?' No one replied. 'Hello?' she repeated. Nothing. 'Bloody prank callers. They ought to be arrested,' she said loudly into the receiver and slammed it down. When she went back into the drawing room, Annetta had fallen asleep in her chair. Her chin bumped her breastbone as she snored. She could sleep through anything.

Light dribbled across the floor like spilt milk. It was evening, but bright, and still so hot outside.

Annetta dreamed of a banquet that lasted all night, long past the sound of the barrow boys calling out what was fresh, what was ripe. A woman's head thrust under her dress, handfuls of hair, then hip to hip, Annetta's breasts with a closed bud on each tip. Lips trembling, holding each other tight.

The pleasure lovers gave; their true and real devotion, unmatched in her since: that complete possession, as when they lay together after and felt the pulse coming in unison, blood coursing in the most secret places of the body.

She saw Nell stretched out in the tin bath, a froth of bubbles ringing her throat like a pearl necklace. All these years she had been missing Nell. She had never wanted her to go. The loss of Nell, the best love she had known, came to her as new and overwhelming as if happening for the first time. It was a good cry, crying for Nell.

Rita shook her awake. 'What's wrong? What's your problem?'

Annetta couldn't say. She tried to get up. Were those her old legs down there? She brushed the cobwebs from them but the pattern of veins remained; the skin was decrepit, bristled. She smoothed her nightdress. *Wet.*

Rita staggered back to the window. She had to keep an eye out. She gripped the sill with one hand, an imaginary drink still in the other. Her lavender wedding suit was dirty down the back and her stockings had run. That fascinator of hers, the curls sprayed hard around it – fixed to her head, feathers twittering with every pronouncement. 'Mr Wye is over there. I swear I saw him in the Rose and Crown on Tuesday.' It could be no other, dressed as he was: a Puritan. 'He's got a camera. He's taking pictures of the house. He's up to no good, I tell you.'

Annetta crossed herself. A man appeared at the door to the room. He was holding a packet of biscuits. Looked like Arthur Gillies, only he'd never been so fat. Mr Gillies was short, solid, bull-shouldered, standing very erect. The man came into the room. Annetta had always been terrified of him. Him and Mr Wye, they'd both been rough and cold, sneaking up on her from behind. They caught her and threw her onto the bed and she knew to give in. She always went limp, easy to handle, silent. Blindfolded, or a pillowslip over her head. Darkness – where she used to go and rest while they did with her what they wanted. All of them, the many men. She looked at Mr Gillies. It was him, all right. She thought she'd die of fright if he took another step. He did. She was gone again.

Joseph saw that Annetta was asleep, head dropped back against the wall. Catching flies, Rita called it, when Annetta dozed like that, right where she sat, in the middle of everything. Sometimes he had to check and make sure she hadn't died, looking so dead, just a sack of skin sagged in her chair. Sometimes he had to really shake her awake.

'Turn up the fire, Joseph. It's cold,' Rita said. He turned it past the 'high' mark, higher than was safe. 'Turn it up, I said. I can feel a draught.'

Joseph turned the knob – it came off in his hand, surprising him so much that he almost dropped it. He looked at Rita. She hadn't noticed, still at the window. He put the knob into his pocket, right where his inhaler should be. He sat down with the packet of biscuits and surreptitiously began to tweak the cellophane, not wanting Rita to chide him for his greed. He slipped in a biscuit and let it dissolve on his tongue, quietly. He gargled, swallowed, palmed a few more and sat back, drawing the rug to his nose and letting it tent from there, eyes just visible above the fringe.

Rita shivered. 'Someone's walking over my grave. There's a real chill in here.' She glanced at Annetta. 'Oh, for goodness' sake. Asleep again! It's because she doesn't sleep at night like the rest of us.'

Annetta was deep inside. She could see better where she was now. Before, it had seemed a wilderness, endless darkness. The sense of a lake in the sky – not seen but there, just heard. Gentle voices, like water. She was on the shore, wading through soft sand. The smell of wood smoke. She saw a cottage she had never seen before, a snug-looking cabin lit from within, its twinkling windows paned in gold. Annetta got closer; her feet knew the path, for she did not stumble in the pitch-dark. She found the door and opened it and said, through parched lips, 'There's that old red dress of mine, hanging just where I left it.' She saw the bed where it should be, not broken in pieces, its eiderdown the very same that she remembered, and a chintz armchair in one corner. She saw a fire where she could warm herself eternally, Nell stretched out before it, burnished by the flames. Nell's ears pricked and she turned eager eyes on Annetta.

'Nell,' Annetta called as she passed away.

'There she goes. Talking in her sleep,' Rita said. 'I can't make out half of what she says any more. Just mumbles.' She tapped the front-window glass. 'Mr Wye is over there. You won't remember him, or maybe you will. He was always about, wasn't he? Your mother couldn't have been nicer. She knew who buttered her bread. Mr Wye and your father were thick as thieves.'

Joseph stopped chewing. Mr Wye? Here? Had he heard her right? Joseph threw off the rug and lumbered to his feet, padding over to see. He peered out at a white-haired old gentleman who stood by the entrance to the park across the way, whose gaze was fixed squarely upon them.

'I reckon he's been there all day. I'm going to have a word,' Rita declared, putting down her imaginary drink to shake a fist at him. 'We have every right to live in this house, I don't care what he says.' With that, she flew out of the room and her fascinator was like a bird caught up behind her.

Joseph backed away from Mr Wye's fierce stare. Rita would sort it out, he had no doubt – she always did. He sat down, fussed with the biscuits, popping in several, maybe four biscuits: a decent pile. He chewed, not enough, for suddenly he felt himself to be choking. The biscuits were going down too slow. Tea didn't help – most of it came splashing back out of his mouth when he took a big gulp, having hit a wall. He coughed. Nothing. Not budging. Another little cough – smaller because he had less to cough. Less, now, for coughing so much. He closed his eyes to conserve energy. Keep his eyeballs in when he coughed, slightly, once more, and collapsed against the chesterfield: capsized again.

He reached into his pocket for his inhaler and pulled out instead the knob from the fire. It rolled from his hand, never to be found. He heard Rita in the front hall, banging around, trying to get the door open. What an almighty row. She swore like a sailor when she was drunk. She'd never hear him.

His lungs shrank, a hellish thing, without the wind blowing in. First one eye glazed, then the other, and his nose dried up in between. The tip of his tongue dabbed at a name: Mama. *Mama.*

Rita opened the front door, ready for war. But Mr Wye was gone.

He had disappeared, as if into thin air. As if he wasn't

really there in the first place. His shadow left no trace, and yet – Rita cocked her head, feeling the change.

The tree branches were still. No taxis ran. The park across the way was empty and silent. Even the gulls and pigeons: not a sound, for once. 'Look at the state of me,' she said to no one in particular, sitting down heavily on the step as the door closed behind her and its lock clicked. 'My good lavender wedding suit, a perfect fright.' She felt for her fascinator – still there, pinned tight. 'I feel as if I've walked a hundred miles.' She made an effort to raise one hand; it floated, white as a flag. Time passed. How much time?

She would rest for a minute then go for help. She had a real thirst on her. Felt like gravel in her mouth. Rita tried to call out, but her tongue refused. Now, that was odd.

It was all behind her, pushing forth. The ants stirred in the dust. She said her true love's name. To want and want and not have: the end of her. The phone rang inside the house – it rang forever more, as far as she knew: ringing, tolling her lot, bleating like a lamb lost, wanting and not having in the cold, in the dark. 'Open the door,' she gasped, as her bones separated and away she dropped.

picador.com

blog
videos
interviews
extracts